ANGEL of the Night

The Monster Within

Cheryl J. Muir

Author photograph by Marissa Morelos of MJ Photography

First published 2016
by Rowanvale Books Ltd
Studios 26-28, Meanwhile House Cardiff
Curran Embankment
Cardiff
CF10 5DY
www.rowanvalebooks.com

A CIP catalogue record for this book is available from the British Library.
ISBN: 978-1-910832-55-4

For every woman who is judged for her strength

And every man who is denied the right to be vulnerable.

Foreword

If you had told me one year ago I would be writing the Foreword for a kinky novel, I would have looked at you as though you were an import from the Planet Crazy.

This time last year I was in recovery from a motor vehicle accident when I sunk into a deep depression. I know this sounds rather somber but bear with me. To escape from the deep feeling of joylessness, I started writing fan fiction and published it under a pen name hidden away in the deep bowels of the internet. I found I enjoyed the experience immensely, and it offered the unexpected benefit of surrounding me with a community of women from across the globe who supported my writing and lifted me up.

As a result of this, my depression started to lift. And as I sat there at the dining room table in my one-bedroom apartment in Vancouver, *Angel of the Night* was born. It hit me like a thunderbolt and ideas flooded to me like a raging ravine. I was filled with an adrenaline and excitement I hadn't felt in years.

My next thought?

I can't write this. I can't write a kinky novel. Don't give this idea to me. Take it away from me.

But the ideas kept coming. I kept writing. *Okay,* I thought. *I will write this book. But I won't publish it. And if I ever did publish it, it would be under a pen name.* Time passed. I became proud of what I had created. I decided to place my name to it. My *real* name (what a radical concept). I hired an editor privately to review the manuscript and support its development, and it turned out I held a strong story in my hands.

I kept writing. It became my therapy. I inserted myself into the wonderful world of Rale. I learned how to shoot a gun to really get into Angel's psyche. I've spent an enormous amount of time in locations frequented by handsome men in suits to absorb Devon's energy (it was all in the name of research, of course). I talked to those in the BDSM lifestyle, and conversed with people who have worked on the peripheries of the sex industry. All of these people are friends of mine, by the way. It's amazing what you learn about the people in your life when you open up to them. And at this point I should mention my rather questionable internet search history – but perhaps that's another story for another time.

In so many ways, this book saved me. I know that sounds corny. But I'm not the same woman I was twelve months ago. I'm stronger and I'm proudly confident in my sexuality. I'm unfiltered. And sometimes I think I'm a little badass. Perhaps I've tapped into Angel. Maybe Angel was a part of me all along.

Here's what I know to be true. Out of my darkest hour came the greatest gift I have ever received.

One closing thought. If *Angel of the Night* piques your interest in BDSM, please do your research first and ensure you play in a way that is safe, sane and consensual. I have gone to great lengths to ensure the play scenes are written responsibly and in a way that is respectful to those in the lifestyle. But the characters in Rale don't always follow BDSM protocol. In short, I would be thrilled if *Angel of the Night* opens your mind and your heart to kink and fetish. But please know this is not a guidebook and it is not intended to be. Play safely.

Finally, whatever turns you on – don't be ashamed.

Stand proud and unleash your inner vixen.

With love and sauce,

Cheryl J. Muir

PS: Want to share your thoughts as you read Angel of the Night? Follow me on Twitter @cheryljmuir and tweet using #AOTN and #TheMonsterWithin.

Unleash the Vixen

It was 2am. The time when she did her best work.

As she walked down the dimly lit alleyway, the only sound she heard was the quiet hum of the city, occasionally punctured by the low rumbling of a nearby passing cab. She adjusted the black leather holster secured to her dark leather coat, her tall, athletic frame tense with adrenaline. She cast a glance over her shoulder. Her ebony hair pulled into a high ponytail, it whipped forwards as she jolted her neck back to center. A notorious assassin working for the Cucinotta family, Angel was forever conscious of those who were out to get her and tonight was no exception.

She turned the corner and stepped onto the main street. Her target's building came into view.

As she entered the stone apartment building on the corner of 5th and Madison, she encountered the doorman, a well-dressed English gentleman decked out in a double-breasted winter coat with gold buttons. He wore a bowler hat and his glasses rested on the tip of his nose. He seemed like a decent, law-abiding citizen by all accounts. Her hazel eyes narrowed as she observed him.

"Shit," she muttered. Access to the service elevator was located inside the lobby with no exterior access point. Security at this time of night was unusual but not unheard of, especially considering the man he was tasked with protecting. *Son of a bitch must have upped security after the bank raid*, Angel mused. On the plus side, the unexpected presence of the doorman would give her easier access to her target's suite. She had planned to use her tools to pick the lock but now she would have keys, a rare luxury. The doorman was senior, with white hair and a kind smile. She approached him and got straight down to business. "I'm here for Fairweather."

The man opened his mouth to speak and took a moment to formulate the words. His voice shook. "Mr. Fairweather informed me earlier that he has retired for the evening, ma'am. May I tell him you stopped by?"

His eyes moved over her, piecing together her intentions. He noted her sleek attire. The gun holster. The belt around her waist with various tools. The tip of a needle visible above the leather. She stepped towards him and he swallowed hard. As she spoke, her tone was chillingly calm.

"You're going to go to sleep. You won't feel a thing. When you wake up, you'll be safe and warm."

The man's mouth moved but this time his fear prevented him from speaking. Before he could react Angel placed her hands around his face and adjusted his neck, rendering him unconscious. Her athletic strength an asset, she dragged him inside the building and placed him on the royal purple couch in the lobby lined with floor-to-ceiling marble. She laid him down on top of the plush fabric and slipped her hands into his coat pocket to retrieve his keys before heading for the elevator.

She reached the penthouse level with ease. Walking out into the hallway, her movements were deliberate. Predatory. She removed her handgun from its holster and held it to the chest of her coat as she traversed the hall like a lioness stalking its prey. Her hand found the back of her utility belt under her coat and she felt for the large needle, primed and ready for use on her target. Reaching the main door, she opened it using the doorman's keys and stepped inside.

The large living space was classic and stylish with an old-world charm, much like its inhabitant. Her target was Devon Fairweather, a prominent businessman and renowned philanthropist. The owner of Fairweather Holdings Group, a financial conglomerate controlling the major financial touchpoints of the city, Mr. Fairweather was a prominent figure in Rale and regularly showcased his charitable efforts in the media. At least, that was the image he projected. Based on her research, Angel knew there was another side of his life he chose to shield from the outside world.

She stalked the shadows throughout his large suite and reached the bedroom.

The room was opulent, which was to be expected. Unlike the light, airy hallway and living space, the bedroom was dark. The rich wooden paneling set the tone of the room, a décor of deep brown leather mixed with smooth cappuccino-coloured fabrics. A pop of colour sat at the foot of the bed – a ruby red chaise with a brown fur throw strewn over its edges. It offset the crisp white linen bed sheets and the deep, rich leather headboard.

Alright, sleeping beauty, Angel thought to herself. *You and I need to have a little chat.*

Only he wasn't asleep. She watched through the crack in the doorway as he sat on the side of his bed, glass of scotch in hand. Despite the unearthly hour, he was dressed in a charcoal grey suit with a matching waistcoat, a pressed dark blue tie and pristine tan-coloured dress shoes. He ran his hand through his blond hair, seemingly exasperated. He looked as though he was expecting someone.

"Alice?" he called out, hearing movement outside his bedroom door. He placed his scotch down on the nightstand and walked towards the sound. Suddenly the door swung open and Angel positioned herself behind him, needle in hand.

"W-what are you doing, who are-"

Angel inserted the needle into the fleshy part of his neck and Devon's vision faded to black.

Using the service elevator, she transported Devon down to a vehicle strategically placed by her aide in the alleyway out back. As she did so, Angel contemplated how her life had changed over the past ten years. It had morphed into something darker than she could have ever imagined.

Interview with the Devil

Angel tapped her foot nervously against the legs of the chair. She found herself sat out in the hallway of Frankie Cucinotta's manor. The mob boss ran the criminal underworld in Rale and was not a man she wanted to irk. She was next in line.

Having lived a life on the streets from her early teens, petty crime was her means of survival. At 19 years old, Angel tried to go straight and she secured a job at a bar. She worked hard to pay the rent on her modest one-bedroom apartment, and it was a constant struggle to simply keep her head above the poverty line. She had made a tough choice. If she was going to have a life in this city and be respected and truly self-sufficient, she had to crank it up a notch. Frankie Cucinotta controlled the entertainment district and the sharp-minded teen soon learned the crime lord owned all of the turf, including The Blackbird Inn where she served cheap beer until the early hours. During a seemingly uneventful shift she overheard a conversation between two of Cucinotta's goons. They were looking for a snitch. She charmed herself into an interview.

And now here she sat waiting to see the man himself. It was her third time at Cucinotta's manor, having met with his two men from the bar in a somewhat official capacity. The hallway sat eerily empty now, such a cruel fate for her to have the last interview of the day. She was sure the mob boss would be irritable, which certainly wouldn't work in her favour.

Inside his office, Cucinotta sighed as he perused her resume. "Really, Dino? *Angelica Rose*? She don't exactly sound like a hardened criminal."

"Don't judge a book by its cover, Frankie," his right-hand reasoned as his stocky physique forced the buttons on his shirt to pull and gape.

The crime lord's tongue roughly lapped the inside of his bottom lip as his brown eyes perused the remaining pages. The content appeared less than impressive to him. It wasn't good enough. Far from it. Frustrated, he screwed the paper up into a ball and tossed it towards his right-hand man.

"She has no fucking experience, Dino. *None*. She's a civilian for fuck's sake. Why should I waste my time with these fuckin' nobodies?"

The mobster's aide cocked his head knowingly. "She interviewed well."

"*Interviewed well*?" The mobster's expression was one of pure disbelief and annoyance. He had reached the end of his fuse. "Look. We're not looking for some doll to look good and take fuckin' notes. This person has to be the best in the fuckin' business. I need them to be my eyes and ears in the city. They have to have skills in fuckin' deception and you know what – seduction. Yeah. Seduction. A fuckin' bar bitch won't have that."

Cucinotta tilted his head back and rubbed his eyes with his left hand. The fingers on his free hand found their way through his thick, dark hair. This morning's shave a distant memory, a shadow formed on the bottom reaches of his face as fresh stubble penetrated his skin. The interview process did nothing to ease his weariness.

"Trust me, boss," Dino assured. "She's got skills."

"Your final candidate, boss," came an obedient voice at the door.

Angel thanked the underling who escorted her into Frankie's quarters. The subordinate bowed his head towards the future assassin as he closed the double doors behind her, believing he was leading a lamb into the lion's den.

Dino looked up at Angel as she walked in. He offered her an encouraging smile. Having taken a shine to her in the second interview, the underboss had advised her to wait until Cucinotta beckoned her to approach him. This didn't happen, and the young crime lord's gaze stayed fixed on his half-empty glass of rye. Dino nodded to her and gave Angel the cue to move forward. Gingerly, she approached the empty club chair in front of Cucinotta, her long black locks tumbling around her shoulders.

"For fuck's sake, I don't have all day sweet cheeks," the crime lord muttered, rubbing his eyes once more.

Angel glanced at Dino for direction. The sidekick's expression indicated her to hurry to the crime lord's side. In seconds she stood in front of Cucinotta, just in time to see him knock back the remainder of his rye. He pushed the empty glass towards the edge of the table and gestured dismissively at Dino: "Get me another."

Angel's hazel eyes were full of fear and panic and she silently pleaded with her ally. *Stay, Dino... please.* Her stomach dropped as he mouthed "sorry" before leaving the room. She noticed the remains of her resume lying in a crumpled heap on the floor next to Cucinotta's chair. *Not exactly off to a good start*, she thought to herself.

"M-Mr. Cucinotta sir, it's such an honour to meet you in person," she started as she attempted to steady her wavering voice, diligently placing down a crisp copy of her resume. "I have a lot of respect for what you have accomplished, and it's my dream to one day be in a position where I –"

He held up his hand and she stopped talking immediately. Finally, he looked at her. "You have no experience."

"Sir, that's true but I work in the entertainment business, in one of your bars on your patch, as it happens. And I've seen a lot. I lived on the streets as a kid, it was tough to get by but I learned I'm able to tackle really anything I set my mind to, and –"

The mobster scoffed.

"Respectfully, sir. Everyone has to start somewhere."

Angel's sudden boldness irked him. His brown eyes burned with rage and his fiery gaze bore into her. He spat: "Give me one good reason why should I hire you?"

"W-well sir," she stuttered again, her nerves reaching an all-time high. "I-I can relate to you. Where you came from. I took the liberty of researching your backstory. I understand your family are immigrants from Italy and you grew up in poverty. Your father, he was a baker. Nobody handed you anything because they didn't have anything to give. You're a self-made man. I relate to that. And I know—" Her voice choked on the words. "I know what's it's like to be prepared to do anything, really anything, to never, ever feel powerless again."

The crime lord understood her story. He noted her stuttering, recalling how he would feel nervous and awkward in his communication with superiors early in his life of crime, while working his way through the ranks. The heartless crime lord had pushed his capacity for empathy deep down in the pit of his gut many, many years ago. He cast her a scornful look.

"Yeah well, that's real nice. If I need a fuckin' motivational speaker, I'll give you a call."

Dino returned to the room and placed a full glass of rye in front of the crime lord. This eased his mood slightly and he took a large gulp of the amber liquid. He flicked Angel's resume towards her. This was her cue to leave. Dino looked at her, eyes pleading, urging her to step it up. Feeling defeated, the teen simply shook her head and turned to leave.

As she walked towards the door, a sudden surge of determination cursed through her veins. She had faced worse than Cucinotta, she figured. *Fuck it. What do I have to lose*? She turned on her heels and walked towards the notorious criminal, ever so slowly. She reached over to his rye glass and placed her hand over his. Still gripping the glass tightly, he looked at her with anger searing through his brown eyes. When he spoke, tiny drops of saliva fell from his pursed lips.

"You fuckin' bitch, who do you think you are."

She ignored him. Gradually, gently, she peeled his fingers from the glass.

"I have skills, Mr. Cucinotta. Skills that are useful to you," she purred, channeling the flirtatious talents she honed night-after-night at the bar.

Ever so slowly, she took his hand in hers, her free hand resting on the arm of his leather club chair before finding its resting place on his thigh. Their faces just inches apart now, she took his hand and lifted it to her face. While looking directly into his dark eyes, she took his index finger in her mouth. Slowly, she twirled her tongue around the outside of his digit. Her resting hand made its way up his thigh. He shuddered under her touch and his face turned from one of fury to a cocktail of emotions Angel had never witnessed before. He was equal parts shocked, mortified and aroused.

His head turned to Dino, who simply nodded

approvingly. Of course, she had demonstrated her skills to the underling during her earlier interview.

Cucinotta turned his eyes back to the olive-skinned beauty in front of him as she took his middle finger in between her ruby red lips. One by one, she simulated fellatio on each of his digits. Her left hand ran up and down his thigh, stopping short of the one place he wanted her touch the most. He was hard. Rock hard. He unbuttoned the top two buttons of his dark grey shirt and wiped the bead of sweat from his forehead with the back of his spare hand.

The crime boss was not short of access to women. He could have any woman he chose to on any given night. But none of them had aroused him this much or this quickly. He shifted in his seat and felt something he hadn't felt in an unfathomable period of time – embarrassment. If she continued the way she did, he feared he couldn't hold back from climaxing. The idea humiliated him to his very core. Used to a position of full control, the commanding crime lord had no idea what to do next. Part of him wanted to tell Angel to stop. Demand her to cease these actions before he had her killed in front of him. The other side of him would do anything to have her finish him off.

Sensing his dilemma and knowing she had proved her point, Angel stopped and placed his moist, warm hand back down on top of his leg. It trembled ever so slightly as it rested against the luxurious fabric. She reached over him and helped herself to a sip of his rye and glanced over at him. She knocked back the contents of the glass and placed it down on the table. Cocking her head to the side, she asked, "When do I start?"

The mobster looked her up and down. He was stunned. She looked innocent, and yet here she was reducing him to a trembling mess. She was a civilian, sure, but that wasn't a problem. It was in fact an enormous benefit. Absolutely none of his rivals would suspect this level of seduction if he sent her to coerce information from them. She was perfect.

Regaining his composure for a second, he spoke, "Alright, Angel-"

"It's Angelica."

"Yeah, well I like Angel better. It suits you," he said, looking her up and down hungrily. "Anyway. You're in. You got the job."

His mouth lingered over the last word and it made her shudder inwardly. The mobster nodded to Angel. It was his signal – she was excused and had his approval to leave the room. Before she turned for the door, she leaned forward and whispered in his ear, "Thank you, sir." These simple words sparked a tingle up his spine. As Dino led her out of the room, Cucinotta called out to her.

"Wait."

Her confident smile fell. The tone in his voice was dark. She turned to face him.

"You're not done, doll. I have your first *job*." He looked at her and glanced down to his crotch, his arousal straining the fabric. She was well aware this scenario was risky. And she had created it. She had played with fire, and now the raging inferno in front of her wanted his release. She looked at him. He wasn't unattractive – early thirties, dark hair, Italian, in decent shape, if not a little rugged. He certainly wasn't someone she would ordinarily choose to be involved with. But he was handsome.

The mobster signaled for Dino to leave and close the door behind him. His aide obliged. Standing up straight and channeling her inner seductress, she returned to Cucinotta's side. She towered above him.

"What would you like me to do?" she asked.

He laughed lowly. “Well, I think we both fuckin’ know the answer to that.”

“I don’t.” She shook her head and forced an innocent smile. She hoped he would take pity on her and let her off the hook. He didn’t. He *couldn’t*.

His guard fell for a moment, his desperation palpable. “Angel. Please don’t tease me anymore. I can’t take it.”

She had to admit to herself – part of the situation thrilled her. The most powerful man in the city sat in front of her on the verge of pleading. Her pulse raced. She wanted to hear him say the words.

“Make me c –” His mouth tripped over the phrase. This was ridiculous. With his wealth and stature, he could have – and he could *pay* – any woman in the city to bring him to completion. And here he sat begging *her*, someone he labeled a ‘nobody’ a mere twenty minutes ago. “Finish me off, Angel. Please.”

Failing to disguise her satisfaction, she grinned wickedly. The power she suddenly held over this man drove her wild and adrenaline surged through her system, overriding her initial gut feeling of fear around inserting herself into a highly volatile situation.

“It would be my pleasure, sir,” she cooed, smiling coyly, confident he wouldn’t hurt her. At least, not until the job was done.

Although unsure if he should utter the next words and allow her into his world for a moment, he decided to take a risk and let her in. Tentatively, he leaned forward and whispered, “You can call me Frankie if you want, Ange.”

A cold shiver ran down her spine. She stood dangerously close to the most feared man in the city. It felt equally terrifying and exhilarating.

“Frankie,” she whispered back, her face once

again inches from his. "It would be my pleasure. Please make yourself comfortable. You must be very tired. Let me take care of you."

He closed his eyes as she reached for the polished chrome buckle of his belt, his mind drifting far, far away from his troubles. This was exactly what he needed.

Slowly, she knelt down in front of him. As she did so, he unzipped his dress pants, his hands shaking ever so slightly. Breathless, he looked at her. "Please. Please, Ange."

She looked up at him with her large hazel eyes as she took his length in her mouth. He cried out a blissful moan and in no less than a minute, he found his release.

Little did she know, the course of Angel's life had changed forever.

The Night That Changed Everything

Angel maneuvered her chrome-coloured town car towards the warehouse in the Northern Quarter located at the top end of the city. She looked up. The exterior of the building displayed flaky green paint and large black letters spelling out 'East Coast Meats', with each letter on a white circular sign. The windows were murky and smashed in at the corners. She had used this space for numerous interrogations and knew every inch of it.

Driving the car into the warehouse and rolling the vehicle to a stop, she popped the trunk and dragged Devon's lean frame out of the small enclosed space. Having bound his hands together in his suite, she dragged him by the roped knot between his wrists. As she hauled her blond prisoner over the uneven concrete floor, water dripped slowly from a broken pipe and echoed in the large space around her. The smell was dank, musty. Cold. She reached one of the only items in the warehouse – an abandoned rack she had positioned in the middle of the floor the previous night – and secured his arms to the meat hooks.

She removed her dark leather coat, adjusted the straps of her black vest and smoothed down her skin-tight leather pants. She removed the balaclava that accentuated her hazel eyes. Now inside the warehouse, she had no need to hide her face. Her fingerless leather gloves remained on. Next, she waited for her target to regain consciousness. She walked around the warehouse, scoping out the space and ensuring nothing had changed since her preliminary visit last night. As she did so, she thought about the job and the person who had assigned her the task. Frankie.

* * *

"That fuckin' son of a bitch!" the mobster yelled, knocking over the contents of his desk with one swipe of his left arm. Angel stood in front of him in his office, having been beckoned to see him. He had insisted it was urgent.

Angel sighed as she crossed her arms, exasperated. Ten years had now passed since her initial interview with the mob boss, and she had spent the past decade working her way up to her current status as the top assassin in the city. An enormous amount had changed since their first meeting and the years hadn't been kind to the formerly handsome crime lord. Now in his early forties, the pressure of running Rale's organized crime circuit had aged him terribly. By any definition of the word, he was repulsive to Angel.

"Frankie, what the fuck is going on?"

"That fuckin' prick at the bank! Fairweather! He set me up! Now the cops are onto me and I'm fuckin' innocent!"

Angel smirked. "Frankie, you're a lot of things, but innocent isn't one of them."

The mobster lunged towards her, furious. "Listen to me. You find Fairweather. You get him to confess and turn himself in. You do whatever the fuck you need to do to get him to say it's him. Understand?"

"Look, Frankie. It's unlikely he set up a raid at his own bank and framed you. My gut's telling me he's not our guy."

"Are you tellin' me you ain't gonna take the job?

'Cause I can find another assassin sweetheart, you're not the only –"

"I'm the best Frankie and you know it," Angel retorted. "Look. My best offer is this. I'll do my research, watch him for the next couple nights, then make my move. But I can't get him to confess if he's not our guy."

Cucinotta nodded dismissively and Angel left the room.

* * *

Back in the warehouse, Devon's eyes opened, the sedation wearing off.

"Finally," Angel muttered under her breath.

"W-where am I..." he mumbled, his vision blurry for a moment. As he became aware of his surroundings he realized his hands were bound together by rope and tied to a meat hanger above his head. His arms already ached from the tension.

"*Mr. Fairweather*," she jeered, walking towards him and mocking his polite English-American diction. "So kind of you to join me."

"What do you want from me?" he asked. His voice was calm and yet his eyes already displayed flickers of anger at his helpless situation. One of the most powerful businessmen in the city, he wasn't used to others having control over him. "Who do you work for?"

"What do I want from you..." she grinned and pursed her lips in mocked thought, toying with her switch blade and resting the tip of the knife on the fleshy part of her thumb. "As for who hired me, well..." She stood directly in front of him now and lowered her voice. "...That's between me and him. Client confidentiality and all that. But. The important question is, why are *you* here and how can *you* help *me*? You..." she whispered, turning around to face him. She leaned in close, her face almost touching his. "You set up the raid at Rale National Bank. Didn't you?"

"W-what?" he asked, nose crinkling and eyes narrowing as he tried to process her words. "*I* set it up? Why on earth would I raid my own bank?"

"Oh don't play innocent with me."

She rolled her eyes and took a step back, crossing her arms and sighing. A moment passed and she leaned in towards him again, her knife pointed at the tip of his nose. Devon felt the sharp sensation and inhaled a shaky breath.

"You set it up. You hired the men, made it look like an inside job. Then you framed Cucinotta."

"Is that who you work for?" he asked, his sharp mind piecing together the details. He had heard the name. "The crime boss?"

"Honey, you're not listening. Now," she cleared her throat and placed the edge of the knife under the area where his neck became his jawline. "Are you going to tell me the truth about the raid, or am I going to have to cut this pretty little face of yours?"

His eyes were wide now, fearful. If his hands weren't tied up above his head, he would have held them up in defence. His voice shook as he spoke. "I-I don't know anything! I swear to you! Please! P-please don't hurt me!"

Angel threw her head back and laughed. A deep, seductive laugh that caused a chill to ripple through Devon's lean frame. Slowly, she ran the knife down the front of his suit, the blade cutting into his Italian silk tie. She pulled at the fabric and the remainder of the garment came loose in her hand. She unfastened the top two buttons of his sky blue shirt and positioned the blade of the knife at the base of his neck once more. His breath hitched and he squeezed his eyes tight shut. His body trembled with terror. And then, all of a sudden, he noticed heat rise in his cheeks and he became viscerally angry.

Feeling helpless was something Devon swore he would never feel again. It took him right back to the night of his parents' death.

* * *

Devon spent his early life in England. His parents raised him in London's Kensington neighbourhood, a location close to the head office of Fairweather Holdings Group. After its inception, the financial conglomerate was initially stationed in the capital. Devon had a happy childhood. While his father worked hard, he always ensured he was home for dinner to talk to his son about his day at school. The young boy felt loved, contented. He didn't know anything else.

The Fairweathers would often visit a national park in the north of England, an area beloved to Devon's mother and father – the Lake District. The rolling hills and endless fields offered a welcome respite from the constant drum of the city and the pressures of running the country's largest financial firm. Devon's Uncle Wallace lived in the region and, a prosperous restauranteur, he owned several establishments beside the lake.

On a clear and crisp December evening, the family of three made their back to Wallace's property in Low Newton after dining at his upscale waterfront eatery. A drive Austin Fairweather had taken countless times, it felt remarkably unremarkable.

"Did you enjoy tonight, Devon?" his mother Isabella asked, turning to look into the back of the town car to see the young boy engrossed in a handheld video game. His mother smiled when she noticed his expression as her only son stared intently at his screen.

"Yes, Mum. Thank you," he said politely as he glanced up at her, not wanting to ignore his mother but determined to complete the level of his game.

"You know, I'll be taking a trip to our Rale office next week my love," Austin explained to his wife as he navigated the winding roads to his brother's stately home. "It's growing rapidly. It very well could become our main office in North America if the markets remain strong."

"You're always talking about work, darling," Isabella said softly. "But I do appreciate how hard you work for us."

As she leaned in to kiss him on the cheek, oncoming headlights engulfed their vision. The last thing Devon remembered was the screeching of brakes and the sound of crashing metal reverberating around their town car.

The death of Austin and Isabella Fairweather dominated the headlines for weeks. Their name prominent in business and philanthropic circles, it was a shock to the country's capital city. It wasn't until many years later that Devon would learn the truth he had been sheltered from – his parents were killed by a group of heavily intoxicated teens on their way back from a night out in a neighbouring village. Devon was the only survivor.

The eight-year-old Devon was unaware of the immediate aftermath of his parents' death, having been knocked into a coma during the collision. One week later, he awoke in the last place he expected. In a hospital bed with nurses at his side.

"Where am I? Where's my Mum? Where's Dad?" the young boy cried out in desperation, his wide eyes searching the cold, clinical room. *Where are they?* The women surrounding him looked at one another, their eyes sad. One of the nurses called for Devon's uncle, who walked into the room with his hat worried between his fingertips. Wallace sat down at his nephew's bedside.

"Devon. I'm afraid... your mother and father... well. I'm afraid they are gone."

The young boy didn't know how long he cried for. The days and weeks passed by in a blur, punctuated only by his release from hospital and the drive to his uncle's home. Devon noticed the large property coming into view as Wallace drove his upscale four-wheel drive vehicle up the stone driveway, the tires crunching underneath them. The once-quaint home now resembled a prison to the young boy sat in the passenger side. This is where he would stay.

Wallace Fairweather had the best of intentions but with mounting responsibilities following Austin and Isabella's death, he didn't have the time or inclination to raise a child. To compensate, he obtained the best nannies money could buy. He showered young Devon with gifts and managed the bill for flying in therapists from London, the very best in their field. To Wallace's chagrin, none of this filled the void his nephew felt from losing his parents. This only fueled the older man's drinking, and he could be found most evenings in his study drowning his frustration in single malt whiskey while little Devon was entertained by the hired help.

When Devon reached the age of 14, he made a bold request of his uncle. He asked to be transferred from his boarding school in the Lake District to a private school in Rale.

"I feel strongly that it's what my parents would have wanted," he insisted, remembering his father's last words.

The reluctant guardian and temporary chairman of Fairweather Holdings agreed, and instructed the company's staff members to chaperone Devon at the airport at both the British and American sides.

Completing his education in Rale was not quite the dream Devon had hoped for, however, and he found himself mocked by the American students for his accent. To cope with feeling ostracized by his peers, he simply buried his head in his books and focused on his work, the only aspect of his life he could control. When he completed his schooling, Devon studied business at the prestigious Rale Ryerson University.

By any estimation, Devon had lived a life of privilege. One he felt grateful for. As he grew into a man, he tried his best to give back and help others less fortunate than himself, and he did so genuinely. It had the unintended consequence of painting him as a pillar of the community, a philanthropist. But he wasn't perfect. Far from it. He was broken. He had never truly healed from the death of his parents.

Devon inherited Fairweather Holdings Group and all its subsidiaries from his uncle. Not once did he take this gift for granted, and he worked tirelessly to maintain his family's empire. There came a time when Devon realized he had invested so much into the business that it had in fact grown far beyond what his uncle was able to accomplish, wildly surpassing anyone's expectations, including his own.

But Devon still felt empty inside. While he filled his days with business matters, his heart sank once the sun set on the city. This is when the women came to visit him. Over the years there were many, many women. He was a handsome, 32-year-old, blond haired and blue eyed millionaire, and he was smart. Smart enough to realize it wasn't him they loved, but the checklist of qualities he so easily presented to them. He treated them well. As well as he could. He was respectful. He never hurt any of them. At least not intentionally, and certainly not physically. Part of him enjoyed the closeness he felt during his time with them. It took his mind off his pain, if only for a moment.

Once his bed partner of choice left for the evening, he would numb his emotions with hard liquor until the sun rose on another day. It was no way to live. Devon knew this. But it was the only life he had ever known.

During his more lucid moments, Devon would observe his reflection in the mirror as he dressed for the day ahead. He noticed the fury that burned behind his eyes. The anger of losing his parents that he had numbed to the point of manageability, but in its place lingered a dull ache in the depths of his soul that he was never truly free of.

He wanted to be a good person. He tried. He really, really tried. But there was a monster inside of him. A monster he fought to tame every day.

Stockholm Syndrome

Devon's blue eyes shot open and he returned to his reality. He shook his head and he was back in the room. His anger, however, went from a slow simmer to a rolling boil.

"I don't know anything! Let me go!" he shouted, shaking his wrists within the meat hooks and trying to free himself.

"Ooh! Someone's feeling feisty," Angel chastised, her eyes widening in mock excitement. She removed the blade from his neck and placed it in its resting place in the leather of her right boot.

"You will pay for what you're doing to me!" he yelled, almost spitting his words at her as his faced reddened with anger.

"Hmm," she laughed. "Funny how a little man in a such a vulnerable position can be so... what's the word... *antagonistic*. What's wrong, hmmm? Angry about your mommy and daddy?"

Before she could say another word he craned his neck back, jolted it forward and spat in her face. Slowly lifting her fingers to her face, she wiped off the sticky residue with the back of her hand, looking down at the dirty concrete floor and then back at him. He *had* to pay. Her silence unnerved him.

"O-oh my gosh, miss, I'm s-sorry," he stuttered. It was completely out of character for him to act in such a disrespectful manner and he offered his apology genuinely. "I-I didn't mean –" His words barely even registered and her arm was already pulled back and ready to strike. She backhanded him with all of the strength she could muster, rendering him numb for a moment. The force caused her hand to sting, offering the assassin an indication of how his face surely felt. His mouth stretched open into an oval O. The shock and pain hit him over and over.

Without another word she walked back to the dusty iron chair in the corner of the room, took a seat and opened the book she had brought with her. It covered the subjects of psychology or, more specifically, victim mentality. Seeing as the opportunity to attend school was robbed from her at a young age, the assassin was self-taught. She selected topics relevant to her line of work and learned everything she knew from the words contained within these pages. She also found that books were a godsend in situations like these when she had time – but not yet a target – to kill.

Devon's eyes narrowed. A criminal, reading a book? He didn't like to judge, but that – *that* he wasn't expecting.

She removed a small razor blade from the middle of the book, where it had kept the next page in place. She found a comfortable place perched on the grimy chair. Fairweather could wait.

* * *

After around an hour, he finally spoke up. He had been coughing furiously for around ten minutes, which evoked attention from Angel but not empathy.

"Miss..." he croaked. "Can I have... some water."

Angel looked up at him. Looking away again, she buried her head back in her book. She hadn't forgotten about his actions and wasn't about to forgive them. Several minutes passed and he spoke up again, pleading now.

"Please... please.... can I have a drink..."

Angel stood up slowly, in no hurry to come to his aid. Her strides were deliberate, confident and seductive. Her heels clicked and echoed in the hollow confines of the open space. She reached his side and took delight in taunting him.

"I'm not one of your servants, *Mr. Fairweather, sir,*" she chastised, fully aware of how he liked to be addressed by his staff.

"N-no. No, of course. But I would be so grateful to you. P-please. C-can I have some water?"

"*Can* you have...? I think what you're asking is *may* you have a drink," Angel grinned slyly. "You know, I would have thought a man who attended the most expensive boarding schools in England wouldn't make such a silly mistake with semantics."

His brows furrowed. *She is surprisingly articulate for a criminal,* he mused. While his experience with organized crime was limited, he was taken aback by her smarts. And her beauty. Her beauty mesmerized him. *Her hazel eyes... her smooth olive skin... the leather that hugged every curve of her toned body...*

His eyes watered, the dust in the disused warehouse hitting the back of his throat painfully. He pleaded with her.

"Please, miss. I'm begging you." He could no longer contain his emotions and to his horror, his eyes glassed over. "P-please..."

Softly and ever so quietly, tears fell down his cheeks. Angel felt an odd sensation in the pit of her stomach. It had been a long time since she had experienced such a feeling but she knew exactly what it was. It pained her to admit it, but she held a small speck of compassion for her target. Dusting off his actions from earlier and realizing she was overly cruel for chastising him for his parents' death, especially knowing what it was like to live without a family, she considered for a moment the scenario playing out in front of her. She had assured Cucinotta that Fairweather was innocent and after her research on the blond, she was convinced her assessment was correct. What would transpire during tonight's interrogation? She would be proven right and she would return to the mob boss to utter a version of, '*I told you so.*' No matter what techniques she used on the man in front of her, the outcome would remain the same.

So she chose compassion. If only for a moment.

"Fine. I must be going soft," she sighed, walking towards the broken pipe in the corner of the warehouse. The cracked metal spewing brown fluid was unsanitary at best and unsafe at worst, but she scooped a rusty tin can from the floor and filled it to the brim with the murky liquid.

"T-thank you, thank you," he stuttered when he noticed Angel walking back towards him.

His hands still tied above his head, she held the makeshift drinking vessel up to his lips. He leaned forward and sniffed the liquid suspiciously.

"I'm not trying to poison you. That's not my style. There are much more fun ways to take care of business." She glanced down at her knee-high black stiletto-heeled boots that held her switch blade. She shook her head. "That's not the point. Do you want this or not?"

He nodded politely and lowered his mouth to the can as she poured the liquid past his cracked lips. He spluttered as the water made its way down his coarse, dry throat. Excess of the murky liquid pooled around his mouth, then onto his crisp charcoal grey suit and now-grimy sky blue shirt. His eyes were wide with gratitude as he looked up at her. He didn't have to say the words. She could sense he was appreciative of her small gesture.

"Don't say I never do anything for you, Fairweather," the assassin said, fighting the urge for her ruby red lips to curl into a smile.

A genuine joke – not like her at all. Angel was all business, using humour only when absolutely necessary as a means to reach her goal and get the job done. Almost instinctively, she used her thumb and wiped away the bloody residue that lingered around his mouth, a result of her succession of strikes earlier in the evening.

"T-thank you, I am so very grateful for your kindness and compassion," he said softly, his big blue eyes looking deeply into her, casting Angel under his spell for a moment. *He's a good-looking guy, there's no denying that*, Angel thought to herself as he continued to show his gratitude. "Truthfully, miss. Thank you."

She stood there for a moment, unsure of what to do next. Hastily she discarded the tin can and allowed it to drop to the floor. The echo reverberated around the empty space, prompting a little jump from her prisoner. She couldn't help but laugh lowly. Yes, he was innocent. But it was still fun to watch him squirm. A well-dressed, powerful man tied up and completely at her mercy? Nothing thrilled her more.

His eyes searched hers. For a second, she saw something behind them. What it was, she couldn't be sure.

"Y-you are quite beautiful. Very beautiful, in fact. You are more beautiful than any woman I ever imagined I would find, I swear I could –"

Angel sneered. His words were genuine, but they angered her. While it was true she used her appearance and sexuality to her advantage, the last thing she needed was another man viewing her as an empty body to be used to live out their sordid daydreams. All of a sudden, she snapped.

"You never miss a beat, do you? I knew you would play this card. You are known as quite the charmer, *Mr. Fairweather...*" Her voice lingered on the end of her sentence, dripping with sarcasm. "That's what you do, isn't it? Pretend to be this nice guy, *'Generous philanthropist Devon Fairweather'*, but it's all bullshit isn't it? I know exactly who you are, how you use women, you –"

"That's not true – well, I-I try to treat them nicely anyways. In any case, that doesn't detract from my compliment. I meant it when I said –"

"Don't cut me off you fucking imbecile!" she yelled, slapping him across the face once more. She gripped his chin between her thumb and index finger, her vice-like grip causing white marks to show beneath his soft skin. "I hadn't finished."

Dropping his head from her hands, she walked away, her back facing him.

"Want to know how I know so much about you? I've been watching you."

"You've been following me all this time? Stalking me?"

"Don't flatter yourself. It was research. I do it with all of my targets. You're not special. You know what I saw when I watched you? I saw those stupid little rich girls come and go, I watched as you screwed them in your fucking penthouse. It's a nice place, you know, I can see why they all go crazy for it. I must say, Devon – *do you mind if I call you that?* – I must say. Everything you've accomplished. It's impressive."

He couldn't tell if she was serious or mocking him again.

"It's impressive... for a weak, pathetic little coward

of a man like you."

Mocking, he mentally confirmed to himself.

Angel turned around to face him and her eyes widened at the sight in front of her. His perfectly tailored grey trousers were... *tight*? His arousal was clear as day.

He likes it, she grinned, delighting in the power she had over him. It wasn't the first time this had transpired during an interrogation, and while she didn't derive any sexual gratification from it herself, she knew many of her targets did. It was wildly effective at getting the job done. But out of all of her victims, she didn't expect this physical response from vanilla-looking Devon Fairweather. Nevertheless, it was time for some fun.

"What the hell is this?" she spat, pointing to the growing peak in his dress pants.

He glanced down, mortified she had noticed. He had felt his slacks tighten and couldn't deny his arousal to himself or his captor. *Why do I feel so thrilled by this woman?* he asked himself. By any standards, his bed partners were physically stunning. But they never turned him on quite like this.

"I-I – well... yes, it would appear this scenario is somewhat... erm... arousing to me. Forgive me. I-I am terribly sorry, I didn't mean to offend you," he replied nervously, his face now burning with embarrassment. He was stunned that he derived such gratification from his vulnerable position, one that was entirely new to him. He certainly never felt so worked up with any of the high society women he succumbed to spending the night with when his loneliness became unbearable.

"Is there a reason you're so... *excited*?" she enquired, grinning slyly.

"Well... perhaps, yes."

"Go on."

He paused. His life could very well be in danger but if this was the way it was going to end, he may as well have this fantasy brought to life.

"Don't keep me waiting," she demanded.

The scenario ticked over in his mind and he thought aloud. "I am feeling there is something rather... exciting... about being controlled. Especially by such a beautiful woman." Angel cocked her head to the side. He was sweet. Pathetic, but sweet. "You are incredibly beautiful, miss."

"Hey, I'm not your girlfriend, sweetheart," Angel muttered.

"No, I realize this, I'm under no illusions about our arrangement." He shook his head as he looked down, defeated.

"Arrangement now, huh? Are you trying to strike a deal with me? You're pathetic. Look at me," she commanded.

His eyes remained fixed on the ground. He was telling her the truth and no matter what he said, she twisted his words.

"Are you deaf as well as fucking pathetic? I said look at me!" she bellowed.

Without question, he obliged as shame filled his fair cheeks. "I'm s-sorry," he stuttered. He was usually so confident with women, but the enigmatic assassin made him nervous. "I am disgusting, you are right. I am so s-sorry."

He inhaled sharply as, without warning, she grasped at the space between his legs, his mouth falling open with desire as he cried out the loudest moan she had ever heard a man emit. She stroked his length through the fabric of his dress pants and he rolled his eyes back as his head tilted backwards in ecstasy.

"You *are* disgusting," she continued, stroking him. "You are sick... twisted... fucked up..."

"Yes... I am..." he whimpered, his eyes still closed.

"You're perverse... warped... abnormal... and most of all, you're *pathetic*..."

Her hands continued to move over his crotch and the feeling overwhelmed him. He was certain he didn't have the stamina to hold on for long. Not only was he physically running on empty from his ordeal, his repressed fantasy was coming to life at the hands of the most beautiful woman he had ever encountered.

He stuttered under her ministrations, "Please stop m-miss, I am about to..."

"About to *what*?" she demanded, already knowing the answer. This wasn't the first time she had used this rather questionable – but wildly effective – interrogation technique.

His eyes shot up and he looked at his captor.

"I'm about to climax."

Her soft lips emitted a sinister laugh. "Imagine this. Devon Fairweather. All dressed up and then coming in his perfectly tailored dress pants." Devon's eyes widened in horror as she used her free hand to pull out her burner cell phone. "I'm sure the video would be worth a fortune," she teased.

For Angel, this was another way of exerting control in order to get the job done. Humiliation was a very powerful tool to extract information. She began using these techniques when she started out in organized crime and, while she initially felt guilty for the hurt she caused, over the years she became numb until she didn't hold a speck of remorse for any of her targets. After all, business was business. The job needed completing. Simple as that. Angel had a reputation for completing the job at any cost and it was a reputation she upheld with tenacity. She had become cold. Ruthless. She liked it that way. No feelings. It was less complicated. And besides, she had done much worse than this.

She looked up at Devon and noticed his eyes roll back. He was close. *So close*. She had to make a decision – should she give him the release he so clearly craved and humiliate him in the process? Or should she deny him his pleasure and save him the embarrassment?

Which option was less cruel?

Disappointed at her inexplicable compassion towards this man, she ceased her movements and stepped back from him as he eyed her curiously. He was a smart man. But he was confused. Did she show him kindness just now, or cruelty? He had no idea. Regardless, he regained his composure and realized how his arms burned from the pressure of being stretched above his head. He winced in pain.

"Something bothering you, Fairweather?" she asked, aiming to ridicule the man further.

"No. No, miss," he responded, shaking his head, all defences gone as his eyes fell to the concrete floor beneath him. His arousal had faded, too. He was genuinely in pain and though it disturbed Angel to admit it, the experience was no longer fun for her. *I'm the one who's disgusting,* she thought to herself. It was one thing to torture notorious criminals, but how could she do this to an innocent man?

She looked at him. His eyes met hers. His blue orbs were glassy. Any hint of the confident, suave bachelor had been stripped away. She swallowed hard and walked back towards him. She was on the verge of doing something she had never done before.

"What do you need...?" she whispered.

He cocked his head and his brows furrowed in

confusion. Was it a trick? She repeated the question and this time he understood. He knew she was sincere.

"My arms," he explained. "I am experiencing a great deal of pain."

Angel nodded and walked towards the corner of the room, picking up the dusty chair that had held her during her reading. She carried it towards him and placed it down in front of him. Expertly, she untied the ropes that bound his hands to the meat hangers. Her face accidentally brushed past his as she reached upwards towards his arms. He closed his eyes, relishing the sensation. He inhaled deeply, taking in her scent. His body tingled, all sensations heightened from the pain he had endured during his capture. His right arm dropped to his side as it was released. His left arm soon followed and, devoid of any remaining physical strength, he collapsed into her.

"I'm sorry, I am so very sorry..." he responded, attempting to steady himself back to his feet.

"It's okay," Angel reassured him, her voice uncharacteristically soft. Wary at first, he allowed his arms to find their place and he wrapped them around her toned shoulders. She helped him down to the chair and he took a seat. "Better?"

"Yes. Much better. Thank you." He smiled at her appreciatively.

She looked down at him. The feeling of concern for him only increased. Despite her better judgement, she decided to reach an agreement.

"Look. I know you have nothing to do with the raid. But Cucinotta expects me to keep you here all night. So we need to stay here and kill some time. I can't let you go yet," she explained.

He nodded. He understood.

Angel toyed with the rope in her hands. Something told her she didn't need to restrain him again.

"You're not going to escape, are you?"

"No, miss," he replied honestly.

She smiled. Her voice softened to a near whisper.

"Hey. Why don't you call me Angel?"

He smiled warmly and allowed her name to roll around his tongue and become familiar. "Angel..." He smiled again, wider than he intended. "I'm Devon."

In spite of the unusual circumstance he found himself in, the entrepreneur defaulted to his corporate conditioning, performing the same action that had closed countless business transactions over the years – he held out his hand to shake hers politely. She accepted, and her lips displayed the beginning of an amused grin.

"Well then," she smiled. "It's nice to meet you, Devon."

The Night Watcher

"He doesn't know anything boss," Angel informed the crime lord as she tossed her leather gloves down onto the small round table. Frankie Cucinotta sat in front of her, glass of rye in one hand and a cigar in the other.

"You sure about that, doll?" he questioned, leaning back in his brown leather club chair. "'Cause from where I'm standin', seems like you have feelin's for this guy."

Angel scoffed, "Frankie, c'mon. Really? He's a target."

"Ah-ah," he stopped her, raising his index finger from the side of his glass and wagging it from side to side. "Remember who you're talking to sweetheart."

"Fine. *Boss*," Angel almost spat, knowing all too well she was now forbidden from using his first name. *I hate patronising this sleazy son of a bitch,* she said inwardly.

Cucinotta shrugged and took another puff of his cigar. He spoke lowly. "I believe ya. I know you wouldn't lie to me baby. I know you too well." His gravelly voice made her shudder.

The mobster tapped the ash from his cigar into the gold ashtray in front of him. Placing the cigar back in his mouth momentarily and placing down his rye, he reached into his pocket and fished out a wad of $100 notes. He counted them out and flung down $4,000 in cash, hesitated, then counted another ten notes. "The extra G is for bein' cute," he added, grinning wickedly.

Angel grabbed the money, uttered a sarcastic, "Pleasure doing business with you," and turned on her stiletto-heeled boots to leave.

"Ya know, *Ange*," the mobster started. Angel stopped, already hating the way this was going. He *always* had to have the last word. She turned around to face him and he continued.

"I'm glad you don't have any feelin's for this Fairweather guy. 'Cause I have another job. If you did like him, well... that would make the job a little tricky for ya."

Angel didn't know what was coming, but she knew it wouldn't be good. "What is it?"

"You're gonna watch him for me. Make sure he's tellin' us the truth and he's not pullin' a fast one."

"I already did my research before the job. I watched him all day and all night. I found nothing relevant. I told you," Angel protested.

"Yeah well, he's a slippery fuckin' fish if you ask me. Don't trust him," Cucinotta insisted. "So you're gonna go watch him for me Friday night. I'll make sure the word is in with his doorman so you don't knock the poor old guy unconscious again."

"How much," Angel spat. It was barely even a question.

"Two Gs, sweet cheeks," the mobster chuckled, before his voice dropped an octave. "Not bad for a night's work, eh?" He had one hand on his cigar and the other dangerously close to the top of his thigh. His brown eyes looked Angel up and down as his hand found its way over the mound in his dress pants. Roughly he grabbed his crotch and sneered at her, "I think about you all the time Angel, you know that? Those sweet lips of yours –"

"Go to hell Frankie!" She lunged at him, drawing her knife over the top of her head. Two of his goons rushed in and held her back as the mob boss leaped to his feet, laughing like a mad man.

"I LOVE a woman with fire!" he laughed, clapping slowly. "Yes!!"

Angel struggled to wriggle free from his goons and instead allowed herself to stay within their vice-like grip. Cucinotta approached her, his face in hers. His expression was stony now. Calm and frightening. He inhaled smoke from his cigar and blew it out slowly into her face. Angel let out a sharp breath through her nose as she suppressed a cough. Her eyes met his. If looks could kill, the mobster would have fallen to the ground right there. She had lost count of how many times she had attempted to end his life. *He's not untouchable*, she told herself. *He isn't God*. But his security was solid. He appeared to be the only life the assassin couldn't take.

Her eyes blazed with anger and yet, as always, her ferocity did nothing to deter the seasoned, powerful crime lord.

"Remember sweetheart," he whispered, "We made a deal years ago. I own you. Now do your job. And get out of here."

Her face contorted into a snarl and she choked out a "fine." His goons loosened their grip on her and she walked out of the mobster's lair.

* * *

Angel rounded the corner of the now-familiar hallway leading to Devon's penthouse apartment. Prepared to pick the lock of the front door, she tried the handle and was surprised to find the door opened with ease. She slipped inside effortlessly.

Devon had purposely kept his door unlocked

every night since his capture. He hoped Angel would return in the dark hours and wake him from this nightmare, this charade. The act of the suave playboy who lived for the pleasure of the many women he spent the night with. The nightmare of a life of opulence that only served to act as a smoke screen between his persona and the monster that resided within him. A monster that lay dormant until he was captured by a beautiful, mysterious assassin who only went by one name. *Angel.*

"*Angel…*" he whispered.

The woman hiding in the shadows peered around the doorway into Devon's bedroom and drew a breath at the sight before her. Devon Fairweather, wearing a navy blue three-piece suit minus his suit jacket, lay on top of his bed, pleasuring himself and whispering her name. A smile crept onto her face as she watched him.

This routine had become a nightly occurrence for the blond. He fantasized about the night he would see her again. He didn't know how it could happen; he had no way of contacting her and no idea where he would find her. But he needed her. Her touch, her intoxicating touch.

Suddenly the clanging of fine china jolted the assassin from the scene before her. She noticed a prim and proper-looking woman approaching the bedroom. She had auburn hair, dressed nicely. Pretty. Mid-twenties. Angel swiftly retreated around the corner and waited until the maid entered the bedroom with the tray of tea. Angel recognized the servant from her research of Devon prior to his capture. She was well aware Devon and his red-haired hired help had a history. Angel had witnessed two occasions where the duo had spent the night together. Clearly their relationship had ceased now, she mused, especially given Devon's current ministrations.

"Alice! Oh, god...!" The blond man sat bolt upright on the bed, hurriedly tucking himself away, his arousal barely able to be contained within the confines of his tailored trousers.

"I'm so sorry, Mr. Fairweather, sir. I should have knocked, I apologize," the maid spluttered, embarrassed by the sight of her boss and averting her gaze as she placed the tray of tea down on top of the chest of drawers. She turned around to face him and finally met his eyes. To allay the shock on the face of the blond man, Alice spoke softly, "If it's any consolation, sir. I have seen you before."

"Y-yes," Devon spoke at last. He swallowed hard. "Yes that is true."

After an awkward moment, Alice turned to leave. "I will leave you be, sir. Unless there's anything else I can do for you?"

Watching through the crack in the bedroom door, Angel rolled her eyes. *There's nothing you can do for him*, she thought to herself.

What happened next made her stomach turn.

"Actually, Alice. There is one thing," Devon started. He removed his tie as he gestured for the maid to step forward towards the bed. He sat up and his legs hung over the side. Obediently, she knelt at his feet. He lifted her chin with his index finger and she looked up at him. He handed the tie to her. "Alice, I need you to be in charge tonight. I want you to tie me up. Using this."

His demure companion shook her head. "Mr. Fairweather, sir, I'm afraid I-I can't do that. I wouldn't know where to start, honestly, I –"

"No. No, I thought not," he responded. "Well. The usual, then."

Of course. Of course she can't. Alice is sweet and

pretty, but she's not her, he thought, sighing. Back to the normal routine of playing the strong, confident, dominant business man. It bored the life out of him, but if it's what he must do tonight to get his kicks, he would. *Angel was right. I am disgusting,* he thought to himself.

He beckoned for the redhead to stand up and she did so dutifully.

"Thank you, Mr. Fairweather. And if I may say so..." She paused, looking him up and down. "You look smouldering this evening, sir."

A smile crept onto his lips. Sure, she wasn't Angel. But she would do the job. On the other side of the door, his night watcher's feet remained rooted to the spot, staring numbly at the sight playing out in front of her.

Devon's usually sharp mind fogged over, clouded with lust, as he surveyed Alice from the fiery red hair on her head to the nude pumps at her feet. Once he managed to formulate a sentence in his mind, he spoke.

"At the risk of sounding inappropriate – you look ravishing, my dear. Please, come."

Smiling, he patted the bed lightly, beckoning for his companion to sit beside him. She obeyed his instructions and fell right into her role.

"Sir, you look awfully uncomfortable. May I help you...?" she asked politely as the blond nodded. He smiled, his tongue darting out and wetting his lips ever so slowly. She sat next to him, leaning over him as she unbuttoned his navy blue waistcoat. It fell to the ground.

"Please Alice, continue."

"Thank you sir, it would be my pleasure."

She unbuttoned his white shirt and untucked it from the waist of his trousers. It too fell away. He sat there now in only his navy blue dress pants, his toned torso heaving lightly as his heart rate increased. He shifted noticeably under her touch.

"Forgive my boldness sir, but your belt must be making you awfully uncomfortable, also... allow me to give you a hand."

She reached down and placed her hands upon the cold chrome of her boss's belt buckle.

"Yes, I could certainly use a hand, my dear," he husked, taking her hand and driving it lower.

Outside the bedroom, Angel's heart started beating irregularly. She blinked, unable to believe the sight. Was this the same man who asked – no, *pleaded* – to be dominated and humiliated? Who swore he had never encountered anyone quite like her and would do *anything* for her touch? The assassin watched as Alice's palm grazed the fine Italian fabric covering his impressively sized arousal. His maid's voice shaking slightly, she whispered, "Anything to serve you, sir."

Soon Devon sat in just his Italian silk boxers, his hands steadying himself on the bed behind him as his torso leaned back at an angle. He sat up and leaned in towards his bedmate. His hand moved its way up from her lower back, his slender fingers teasingly stroking her skin under the fabric of her white chiffon blouse until his digits stopped at the lock of her bra. He unhooked it roughly.

She gasped audibly as he ripped open the front of her blouse, taking her bra and several pearl buttons with it. Exposed now, she looked down at her breasts and looked back up to Devon. With unyielding passion, he buried his head in her curves and roughly planted kisses all over her chest. His lips were hot, wet, feverish. He desperately covered every inch of her, devouring her, hungry for more. Breathless, he continued his mission to take his mind off the woman who had plagued his fantasies.

Alice moaned, her head tilting back in bliss. Suddenly Devon changed his plan.

"Pleasure me," he husked, running his fingers softly down the space between her breasts, "My sweet, sweet Alice."

Alice nodded and knelt at his feet once more. He shifted towards the edge of the bed and spread his legs wide. At the first sensation of her mouth on him, he moaned. Over several insanely pleasurable minutes, she worked him into a frenzy. Angel looked on, feeling a mixture of emotions she couldn't place a name to.

"S-slower, slower..." he gasped out, dangerously close to the edge.

Tempting though it was to finish him, obediently Alice slowed the pace. After several more minutes, he commanded again.

"Harder."

Playing her role as the good little servant, she did as instructed. Sensing he was reaching his peak, he moved forward and ran his fingers delicately through her silky hair.

"Alice," he stuttered out, feeling warmth spread throughout his body. "Do it."

She knew what was required. She worked her hands, lips and tongue in unison and brought his gasps and moans to a crescendo. His climax spread through him like a wildfire and he felt as though he would explode with pleasure.

He was breathless for a few moments, and she respectfully tucked his modesty back into his silk boxers. Once he regained his composure he leaned forward and whispered to her.

"You have performed your duties to my satisfaction. Now. Stand."

She stood up from her kneeling position and, as she stood, Devon reached up and ripped off what was remaining of her blouse. He would buy her a new one. The dogtooth-patterned pencil skirt fell away next, along with her white lace panties. Only the stockings and heels remained.

"Lie down."

She lay down on top of his fine bedsheets and awaited his instructions.

"Relax for me Alice," he whispered, his voice soothing now, a stark contrast to his domineering tone earlier. This was the tone she loved so much. "It's time for you to be pleasured. I will delight you..." he placed kisses on her chest once more... "enrapture you..." his hands moved down past her navel, his mouth following, "I will ensure..." he breathed heavily in between the kisses he planted on her skin, "your good behaviour is rewarded. I will give you your release. It's your turn now. I will treat you like the queen that you are..."

His hands and mouth reached her femininity, noticing she was more than ready for him.

It was too much for Angel to handle. She bolted out of the suite, and with anger coursing through her veins she slammed the penthouse door shut behind her. Devon sat upright in bed and immediately leaped away from his mate. He knew. He knew it was her.

"Shit," he cursed, stepping off the bed and frantically searching for his clothes. "Alice, I'm sorry, I –" He look*ed a*t his maid. He didn't want to hurt her, but he also couldn't waste any more time and risk Angel getting away, never to be seen again. As he stepped into his dress pants and haphazardly threw on his shirt, he mumbled, "I'm sorry Alice. Just, umm, take the night off, okay? And the day, tomorrow. I'll pay you, don't worry. I'm sorry, but I have to go."

He felt like a coward as he darted out of the apartment and left his bedmate naked and alone. His shirt open, he roughly buttoned it up as he pressed the button to call the elevator. He noticed the LED display of another elevator making its way to the ground floor. The red letters displayed the floors it passed. *20, 19, 18...* closer and closer to the lobby and the exit. “Come on, come on, hurry...” he urged as he pressed the elevator call button repeatedly.

Outside, Angel sprinted into the alleyway. She stopped when a feeling overtook her completely. Placing her hand on a metal garbage can to steady herself, she leaned over and emptied the contents of her stomach into the gutter.

Just seconds behind her, Devon exited his apartment building and looked frantically from left to right. *Where would she go? The alleyway*, he thought logically. He ran as fast as he could, but when he reached the alley, all that remained was the memory of her. She was gone.

Two Separate Worlds

Angel stormed through the red doors of The Blackbird Inn, walking up to the bar and pulling up a stool next to an intimidating-looking bearded man clad in biker gear. Teddy. A high-ranking member of Rale City's chapter of a notorious motorcycle gang, over the years Teddy had stepped in as a mentor to Angel, and in many ways she saw him as a father figure. She trusted him with her life, something he had saved on more than one occasion when she started serving drinks at the dingy drinking hole.

"What's eating you?" Teddy said, looking up from his beer as Angel sat down next to him. The bartender slid her a large measure of triple-distilled neat vodka in a tumbler and she knocked it back.

"Nothing I can't handle," she responded, offering her friend a small smile.

"You sure? I'll put a cap in him, whoever he is."

Teddy cracked his knuckles, tattooed with four letters that spelled out 'ANNE', his late wife's name. He knocked his neck to one side, eliciting a cracking sound, and he jolted his elbows sharply back to stretch his back, warming up for a confrontation that would never come.

"It's alright Teddy," she assured him, her voice softening now. "You can stand down. But thank you."

* * *

Devon's tongue lapped the inside of his cheek as he sat at the head of the table in the chic boardroom.

The floor-to-ceiling windows allowed light to stream in and fill every inch of the room, the view outside overlooking the city skyline and offering breathtaking views of Rale. But it didn't matter to Devon. The board meeting never seemed to end and the financial mogul's mind was focused on anything but business today. He couldn't stop thinking about Angel and how epically he had screwed up. He had to find her. He *had* to. His chin rested on his thumb, his index finger finding its place on the side of his cheek and his remaining digits grazing his lips.

"Mr. Fairweather?"

Devon looked up, shaking the thoughts from his head for a moment. He barely heard his Chief Financial Officer.

"Mr. Fairweather, are there any other matters to be brought to the board's attention?"

"No, Charlie. Thank you."

The blond nodded at the table packed full of executives and they dutifully filed out. Two people remained – Mike and Will, Devon's security detail. They were recent hires, both of them coming with a hefty recommendation from Devon's uncle back in England after he heard of the raid at his nephew's bank. His two aides were incredibly different from one another. Mike was solidly built, medium height and rough around the edges. He had short brown hair, a broad Manchester accent and a gold chain permanently fixed around his muscular neck. His application for the role explained how he was discharged from the British army after serving overseas, brute force his modus operandi. Will, on the other hand, had a radically different approach – excelling in the British secret service, he was clean-cut, intelligent, refined and methodical.

When Devon noticed the final board member

filing out, he gestured for Will to close the door and beckoned them both over to him.

“I have a job for the two of you,” he started. “It’s rather... sensitive... in nature.”

“Yes of course, Mr. Fairweather,” Will replied.

“What is it, boss?” Mike choked out. Will rolled his eyes at his counterpart’s gruff delivery.

Devon’s eyes glanced to the right, then the left, scanning the room as if the walls had ears. He shifted in his chair and cleared his throat. Finally, he spoke.

“I need you to find someone.” His aides nodded. He continued. “Unfortunately, I don’t know an enormous amount about her. I *do* know she works for Frankie Cucinotta of the Cucinotta crime syndicate. She works as an assassin, primarily during the night. She goes by the name of Angel.”

Mike let out a thunderous roar of laughter, prompting a perturbed glance from Will.

“Something funny, Michael?” Devon spat, glaring at his bodyguard. Mike’s laughs gradually subsided and he explained his amusement through muffled chortles.

“Sorry boss. It’s just – she’s not real. I mean, people talk about this Angel. But she doesn’t exist. She’s like a – an urban legend or something. Sounds nuts, anyway. Some fit bird kidnapping men from their beds in the middle of the night? I mean, c’mon!”

Devon cocked his head and responded to the burly man, “I assure you Michael. She’s very real indeed,” he paused, unsure if he should share the following revelation. “I’ve met her.”

Until now, he hadn’t uttered a word of his capture to anyone, even going to the lengths of assuring his doorman George that nobody had entered his penthouse the night of Angel’s visit, despite his doorman describing a dangerous-looking woman who had rendered him incapacitated for the majority of his night shift.

"Met her have you?" Mike mocked.

"Forgive my comrade," Will interjected. "What he means to say is, what is your connection to this individual and –?"

Devon wasn't listening. Sighing, he rose from his black leather chair and walked to the dark wood credenza located at the back of the boardroom. He opened the cabinet door to reveal a safe. Expertly entering the dial combination code, Devon fished out several wads of crisp notes. He returned to his seat and stood beside it, placing the two stacks of notes on the end of the boardroom table in front of the two men.

"Perhaps this will convince you she is not a figment of my imagination."

Mike raised an eyebrow. Will asked, "What other details do you have? Her appearance, any distinguishing or prominent features?"

Devon thoroughly explained Angel's physical features, remembering every last detail. He did so with ease, her image seared into his memory. The two aides collected their cash and turned to leave the room. Before they exited, Devon added, "Gentlemen. This must stay strictly confidential." They nodded.

Over the coming days, the two unlikely partners in crime roamed the city and used their various techniques to track down the dark beauty. Several nights in a row they located her at a renowned criminal watering hole, located on the edge of the Brewery District. Having reported her whereabouts to their employer, Devon decided he would visit the establishment with support from his security.

Devon waited until the sun set before he made his way to the bar, flanked by Mike and Will. During the departure from his building, Devon checked his reflection in the mirrored walls of the elevator. He was dressed in a finely tailored navy blue suit with a light blue tie, an accessory he adjusted repeatedly. He had to look immaculate for her. In his mind, it was absolutely essential.

The two security guards escorted the entrepreneur to his private underground parkade and drove him to the establishment where he would find her. The trio exited the car and made their way towards the bar. Devon surveyed the dark grey exterior and its red brick trim below the red neon sign displaying its name.

"The Blackbird Inn? Are we sure this is the place, gentlemen? It seems rather... quaint," he reasoned.

"This is it, boss," Mike assured him. "That assassin bird is here all the time. Hangs out with some biker type at the bar. You're right you know – she *is* fit."

"That's quite enough, Michael," Devon demanded as they reached the red double-doors of the watering hole and stopped.

Devon's heart started pounding. His energy occupied with the hunt, the usually calm, rational businessman truly hadn't thought through his next steps. All he knew was that he must see her. To talk. To explain. He pushed the doors open and walked into the dark, musty tavern with his aides following closely behind. The bar's patrons looked up at the financial mogul and his security detail, their crisp attire a stark contrast to the dingy space. Devon internally begged for one set of eyes to look up at him. And there they were. A pair of hazel eyes. They grew noticeably wide upon seeing him.

"He's with you? That Fairweather guy?" Teddy asked Angel, cocking his head towards the blond. A prominent figure in the community, Teddy easily recalled the name of the man in the sharp blue suit and, knowing her well, he noticed Angel's expression change when she saw the well-dressed man stood in the doorway.

Devon's face beamed when he saw her. She was even more beautiful than he remembered. He walked towards her. She remained perched at the bar, her body now turned to him as her face began to glaze over in anger. Looking at him triggered the memory of the graphic scene she had observed in disgust just several nights prior. Devon noticed her stony expression, but he continued walking towards her, persistent in his mission to explain his actions.

"Hello Angel," he started, reaching her side. He looked down at the floor and placed both hands in his tailored pockets. "I-I thought I might find you here. I-I wanted to speak with you. If I may."

"No. Go fuck yourself," she dismissed, turning her back to him.

He reached forward and hesitantly placed a hand on her shoulder. "Angel, please. I know it was you in my suite several nights ago. I know what you witnessed was ghastly. And, well... I'm so terribly sorry."

Without more than a second glance at him, she abruptly rose from her seat, storming out of the back exit of the bar and out into the dimly lit alleyway. Devon swiftly followed her. Unwilling to get involved in what revealed itself to be a deeply personal matter, his sidekicks stayed in the bar.

"Angel, please. Allow me to explain, I –"

Out in the open air of the darkened alleyway, illuminated only by small spotlights from nearby street lamps, she spun around to face him. Her nostrils flared. Undeterred, he continued.

"Angel, I'm sorry. It was a moment of weakness. It doesn't justify my actions, but please believe me when I say I thought of you every night." He looked at the ground once more, shame filling his fair cheeks. "If you only knew how many times I found my release with your name on my lips. I swear to you, Alice holds no real importance to me, I –"

"You think I give a fuck? You're nothing to me!" she screamed.

"I know that's not true," he said calmly, his eyes piercing into hers. He saw right into her soul and it terrified her. "I know it's not true, Angel."

Violence her default reaction, she lunged at him, pushing him against the brick wall and pinning him in place with her body. She deftly removed her switch blade from her boot and held it to his throat. "Give me one good reason why I shouldn't spill your guts right here?"

Rational thinking completely gone, Devon made a sudden movement – he grasped her face with his hands and pulled her lips onto his. His grip was almost vice-like, his kiss aggressive. Hungry. The action took the assassin completely by surprise, prompting her knife to fall through her fingertips onto the dirty ground beneath her. His tongue begged for entrance and she slowly parted her lips and allowed her eyelids to close. She gave in to the sensation of his kiss.

A chaotic wave of thoughts raced through her mind, and she instantly summoned a host of reasons why she shouldn't allow this man to continue his movements. Despite this, he felt her body ease into him and he loosened his grip. He softly cupped her faced now. She tried with all of her might to suppress it, but a soft moan escaped her lips and she groaned into his mouth. Though it pained her to admit it, she knew his words were absolutely correct. He *was* something to her. She didn't know how to label him yet, but she felt her walls breaking down. She kissed him back, more forcefully now. He tasted like heaven.

Devon placed his right hand on the mid-point of

her back and firmly moved her towards him, closing the gap between them until their bodies pressed up against each other. He could feel the heat of her body on his chest as he tasted her. She was everything he imagined. His mind went to some interesting places, racing from all of the things he wanted to do to her – throwing her down on his bed and pleasuring her until she felt faint – through to his dark desire for the things he would let *her* do to *him*. Above all else, he couldn't believe how fortunate he was to be wrapped in an intimate embrace with the woman of his fantasies. The same woman who, little more than seven days prior, was on the verge of ending his life.

Suddenly, she placed her hand on his chest and pushed away from him. The emotions she had started to feel were simply too overwhelming. Before he could protest she swiftly scooped up her knife from the ground and ran down the alley away from him, her steps echoing off the concrete walls surrounding her.

He immediately started to run. He chased her for the length of the alleyway, but his physicality was no match for her athletic prowess and she sprinted into the night before he could reach her.

On his slow walk back into the bar, he noticed a card on the ground. *It must have fallen from her boot when she removed the knife*, he figured. He picked up the small item and noticed the matte black cardstock with silver glossed lettering. It displayed only one letter, and beneath the single digit sat a harsh stylized underline that resembled a slash from a knife. Devon looked at the reverse of the card and was bewildered. It was blank. No contact information. Nothing.

The only content on the small black card was one simple letter:

"A."

Protected

"Find anything useful?" Frankie asked as he puffed on his cigar, his rough fingers counting out Angel's cash.

"Nothing related to the raid, if that's what you're asking," Angel spat. She now realized exactly why Frankie had sent her to watch over Devon. He didn't admit to it of course, but she knew it intuitively. The mob boss wanted her to see the infamous blond womanizer caught in the act. The crime lord knew Angel had a soft spot for her target and he would do anything and everything in his power to kill whatever bud of hope he saw blossoming in his prized assassin.

Frankie laughed, "Well that's not what I asked, is it sweet cheeks?" He tossed the cash on the table and Angel picked it up. She stared at him, her contempt for her boss rendering her speechless. He looked up at her, his eyes dark, sinister. Her stomach lurched at the crime lord's next words.

"Me and my boys might have to pay him a little visit."

Angel knew the best course of action was to show no emotion in Frankie's presence. She suppressed her desire to defend Devon and profess his innocence. Instead, she shrugged and feigned disinterest. "Whatever you need to do. Business is business."

Showing zero emotion, a skill she had finessed over the years, she told him what would happen next. "Frankie, I won't be taking on any more jobs for you the next couple weeks. I have other contracts."

"*Other contracts*? You fuckin' kidding me?" the

mob boss roared, leaping from his leather club chair. The thought of her working for another gang was intolerable to him.

"It's just for the next couple weeks Frankie. That's all," Angel assured him, lying convincingly. Because of their chequered history of closeness and conflicts, she knew what worked on him. She flashed her megawatt smile and dialed up her levels of seduction while purring, "I'll come back to you, I promise."

He simmered down. He had no idea she was lying to him, but as his eyes roamed over her curves, he truly didn't care.

"Alright doll. I'll call ya when a job comes in."

She nodded and turned to leave. As she walked through the long hallways of Frankie's manor, she thought about the threat he had made to Devon's life. No matter what had transpired with Devon and his maid, Angel knew he was in grave danger. She felt responsible. It was her duty to protect him.

The following night, Angel finished up a contract killing in an abandoned mill in the Northern Quarter. As she wiped the blood from her knife, she made her way back to The Onyx, a boutique hotel in the financial district. It was her temporary abode. The term *home* would be a stretch – it was simply a place to rest her head until it was time to move on again. She entered the hotel building through the loading dock in the alley, and quietly made her way up the emergency stairwell onto the 11th floor. The door opened out into the hallway, just two doors down from her room. She turned the key in the lock and, looking over her shoulder, she let herself in.

Her nightly routine, Angel searched her room for any signs of entry. She checked the table-top ice bucket, stashed full of her cash. Not a note had been touched. Her weapons remained in the back of the closet. It was all clear.

"For fuck's sake."

The only problem was the coffee machine. It stared back at her, minus the pouch of pre-made coffee ground. A long night ahead of her, she needed her fix and was on the verge of calling her trusted aide when she heard a knock at the door. Peering through the spy hole first, she opened up.

"Sebastian. You're a gem," she grinned at the young night porter and grabbed the coffee pouches from him. He nodded and left her to her business. She would summon him when she needed him again.

Sebastian was no ordinary night porter. He was working his way through the rungs of organized crime and, while currently low on the totem pole, he was of great use to the assassin. He was her assistant of sorts, running errands for her, picking up ammo and renting vehicles for contract killings. He would even drive the vehicles away from the kill site so she could concentrate on what she did best. He was young and while experience and intellect were not on his side, he had a certain charm about him. Above all, he was discreet. She trusted him.

After fueling up with the warm black nectar, Angel walked the short distance to Devon's building on 5th and Madison.

"Good evening, miss," George smiled as Angel approached the front door. They had formed a bond after her second visit to Devon's penthouse. That night, she had explained she had no intention to hurt Devon, and George believed her. And while Devon denied ever meeting the spunky assassin on the night of his capture, after the recent debacle at The Blackbird Inn, he decided to give his doorman specific instructions to grant access to a woman matching her description.

Angel smiled at the kind man. “Listen, George – I’ll be here for the next couple of nights. I’ll need access to Devon’s suite. Would you be able to help me?”

He nodded. “Of course. Nothing to be alarmed about, I assume?”

Angel took a breath. She told him the truth. “George, I-I think someone wants to hurt him. A very dangerous man. So I’ll be here. Until the threat has passed.”

George nodded. He informed her of Devon’s two new hires, his security detail. Angel pieced together the information and realized they matched the description of the two bodyguards accompanying Devon when he entered the notorious watering hole. From George’s generous explanation, Angel learned the security duo stayed with Devon during the day, ever present and aware of the dangers that came with the dubious honour of being one of the most powerful men in the city. This left an obvious gap when the sun went down and, wise though George was, he was no match for Cucinotta’s goons.

She would watch Devon during the night, she decided.

“George, I’ll need your keys. Is that cool?” Angel asked.

“As it happens ma’am, I took the liberty of cutting you an extra set.” The kind man smiled and handed her the keychain.

She thanked him and made her way up to the 32nd floor using the main elevators this time. She reached the front door of the penthouse and was surprised to find that, once again, it was open. *Someone needs to tell this guy to lock his door*, she thought to herself.

Quietly, she crept inside. She found him comfortable and asleep in his bed. She smiled.

Over the coming weeks, this became Angel's nightly routine. The times would change from night to night, juggling her contract work around her new role as Devon Fairweather's anonymous protector. She stood guard at his bedroom door, listening intently for approaching footsteps in the hallway. Footsteps that, unbeknownst to her, would never come. Some nights, Angel would walk into Devon's bedroom, standing in the threshold before finding her place on the large red chaise in front of his bed. She would watch him sleep. It calmed her somehow. There were evenings when he would stir, almost waking but never fully coming around.

Since the night in the alleyway behind The Blackbird Inn, he dreamed about her every night. In the surreal state between sleeping and waking, he often saw her at the foot of his bed. She would be smiling, happy. Peaceful. He swore he could smell her, hear her breath. So vivid were his dreams. One night, he started to wake and he felt her presence. He woke slowly, but his eyes remained shut. He was afraid to open them. Afraid she would disappear, a dream once more. She saw him stir and she remained on the chaise in front of his large king bed.

"Is that you...?" he whispered, his eyes still closed.

"Yeah," she said softly. She smiled. A warm, genuine smile. Quietly, not wishing to disturb the semi-conscious man, she stood and walked to his side. She sat down. He felt the weight of her body on the side of his bed, felt her presence so close to him. Finally, he had enough belief in this illusion to open his eyes. That's when he saw her. She was sat close enough to almost fill his field of vision, and the moonlight peeking through the curtains illuminated her, surrounding her in an iridescent light. She glowed. It took his breath away.

"You're really here," he said in a soft, hushed tone, reaching out to her as he sat upright. He touched her face. She smiled, warm and soft. Several moments passed, and her expression changed. To one of concern, of worry.

"Devon. I need you to listen carefully. I've been here recently. Keeping watch. You're in danger. Frankie, he – he's losing his mind. I've brought you something to protect yourself. You need to keep it with you at all times."

He looked at her numbly, struggling to comprehend her words. Unconvinced he had grasped the true gravity of the situation, she asked him, firm but kind, "Do you understand, Devon?" He nodded.

He sat up and she gently pushed him back down into his bed, glancing at the light of his clock on his nightstand. 3:30am.

"Go back to sleep. It's late. I'll leave it here."

Devon protested, but his sleep-addled brain couldn't compute a convincing argument.

Later that morning his alarm rang and, with weary eyes, he reached over to end the shrill sound drilling into his skull. He rubbed his eyes. Another dream about Angel. He sighed. He took a second look at the nightstand and that's when he saw it.

A silver pistol with a note:

Devon,
Use this when I'm not here.
A.

Out of the Darkness

Devon adjusted his tie as he looked at the mirror in front of him. His reflection had changed over the past couple weeks. He physically appeared more rested, a testament to the nights he spent asleep in his bed rather than burning the midnight oil with his *love-interest-du-jour*. There was a quiet confidence to him now. A certainty. A deep knowing that everything was going to be okay. It made no sense on a logical level. Rale's mob boss wanted his head on a platter and the only person preventing that from happening was a ruthless assassin he barely knew. An assassin who crept into his apartment every night and watched him sleep.

He looked at his reflection once more. He wasn't sure who this new man was. But he certainly liked him a whole lot more than the caricature he was used to seeing staring back at him. Taunting him. Reminding him of the lie he was living.

"Angel?" Devon called out as he heard the click of the front door. "Angel, is that you?"

He pushed the fabric of his crisp shirt back to reveal his watch. 7:30am. This was late for the woman who solely operated in the depths of the night. He called out again.

"Angel, you are welcome to come in."

And there she was. He looked up at his reflection and this time he saw her standing behind him. A sight so beautiful it almost took his breath away. Was she real? Was this a ghost staring into the mirror? After what felt like an eternity, she spoke.

"How did you know it was me?"

He stopped for a second. He furrowed his brows, pursed his lips in thought. He glanced his eyes downwards and shook his head. How *did* he know?

"I-I don't know." He looked up at her as he struggled to form the words. "I just... I just knew."

Turning around to face her, he reached out and gingerly placed a hand on her arm. He felt the leather beneath the gentle grasp of his fingertips.

"I want you to know, Angel. I want you to know you're always welcome in my home."

He offered her a smile. A nervous but genuine, warm smile. On the outside, Angel stayed unaffected, although she felt his warmth radiate through her. She glanced at his hand on her arm, and glanced back up at him. His touch felt... good.

"I-I-I am so sorry. I'm sorry, I-I shouldn't have placed my hands on you. Please forgive me, Angel, I –"

"Devon, stop," she whispered, placing her hand over his. Her voice was gentle. "You don't have to be afraid of me." She paused. She cleared her throat before she uttered words that felt so alien to her and yet they rolled off her tongue effortlessly. "I promise you. I won't hurt you."

Devon's smile spread throughout his handsome face, his blue eyes lighting up, his gasp letting out a staggered, "O-ohh..." There were no words he could muster. He appreciated her kindness more than he could express.

She stepped forward, pressing a kiss to his cheek. A simple gesture, but a significant one when delivered from a woman so violent. He held his hand to his face, his skin tingling from her touch. And then she was gone.

The following morning, she appeared again. This

time it was 8am.

Devon sat sipping his tea in his lounge room, the deep brown leather of the wall-to-wall couch keeping his toned physique upright. He sat with his right leg bent, the heel of his right foot resting on his left knee. He placed his tea down on the polished wood table in front of him. He felt something in him shift. He looked up. And there she was once more.

Devon felt good today. Confident. Jovial. A wry smile curled up the right side of his mouth. He placed both feet flat on the floor and spread his arms over the back of the couch. Checking his watch purposefully, he spoke.

"You know I'm still not used to seeing you in daylight hours."

She cocked her head and smiled. "And why's that?"

"Well. You're the *Angel of the Night*. I assumed if you appeared in direct sunlight you would burst into flames."

Angel threw her head back and laughed. A hearty, genuine laugh. She had no idea Devon had a sense of humour. She continued snickering. There was something about his off-beat English delivery that she found incredibly humorous. After a few moments, she composed herself.

"You know it really wasn't *that* funny," he retorted, tipping his head towards her.

"Devon. That was pretty damn funny."

He looked her up and down, his tongue teasing the corner of his mouth. She wore a lace bodysuit, almost entirely opaque aside from strategically placed leather panels. It was quite the risqué attire, even for the ever-sensual assassin. Devon shook the thoughts from his head and asked the most normal question he could muster.

"Good night at work, darling?"

Angel let out a short breath through her nose, stifling another laugh, this time prompted by the normalcy of his question in relation to her bizarre line of work. "You could say that. I had a particularly tricky target tonight."

"Oh...?" Devon asked, his blue eyes curious. "And did you get what you needed from him?"

She shrugged, "Not yet. He's still there. I'll be going back soon, but I had time to kill, so... here I am."

His thoughts raced through his sharp mind. *It's not the middle of the night and she has no need to protect me. She left a target to come here.* His eyes narrowed as he observed her. *She wanted to see me.* It struck him with disbelief. But it was so obvious to him. He stood up and walked towards her. Reaching her, he placed both of his hands either side of her body, his hands finding their resting place confidently on her arms. He had a proposition for her, and paused for a moment as he found the right words.

"My dear Angel. I would like to invite you to stay here today. To sleep. I have no doubt you are able to take care of yourself, but I would feel much better knowing you're here. And safe."

She smiled wide.

"That would be..." What was the word. "Nice. That would be nice, Devon. Thank you."

They looked at each other for a long moment. Devon was the one to break their gaze, walking back to the table to pick up his tea and take a sip. He verbalized his thoughts. "You can sleep in my bed. I'll have one of my staff change the sheets for you, I –"

"Why, what have you been doing in there?" Angel quipped, prompting Devon to turn around and blush furiously. He placed down his tea before he spilled it over his crisp white sleeves.

"I-I-erm... nothing, I-I simply thought it would be the right thing to do for you, I'm sorry, I – "

"Devon, relax. I'm just joking."

He looked up at her. "Very well. I'll have my staff take care of it while you're out."

Suddenly Angel's lips pursed together and anger washed over her face at the thought of the maid who would find her way into his bedroom once more.

"Alice?"

"Oh no, no, no," Devon assured her, walking back to her and he waved his hand dismissively. "No. Alice doesn't work here anymore."

"You fired her?"

"I transferred her to another area of the firm. She – she didn't need to be penalized for my bad choices. She wasn't at fault, Angel. I was. It was my fault. And, for what it's worth, I haven't had any company since that night. Only you."

Angel stared at him numbly as her hazel eyes glassed over. She nodded. The way Devon looked at her, his blue eyes penetrating the very reaches of her soul. He saw right through her, past her exterior and through to the human being underneath the layers of leather. Tears threatened to spill from her eyes but she blinked them back. *What's wrong with you*? she chastised herself.

In one swift movement his body lunged towards her, his hands cupping her face as he pressed his lips to hers. She didn't fight back. She felt dizzy. Overcome. Her mind started swimming with the possibilities, the realities. *He's a civilian. He's not cut out for this life. What am I doing? I can't, I can't...*

"I-I have to go..." She gave him a small smile and pulled away from him. Before making her way back to the warehouse to her awaiting target, she turned as she reached the door and called out to him.

"I'll come back."

And she did. After the kill later that morning, she found herself covered in blood spatter as she walked towards Devon's building. She knew the way up and she found the front door predictably open. She turned the latch and locked it once inside. As she made her way to the bedroom, she found a freshly-made bed displaying a neatly folded white bathrobe, a soft white towel and an envelope with an "A." written on the front in blue ink. She opened it and found a handwritten note on thick, luxurious white cardstock.

Welcome to my home. I'm glad you're here. D. x

She flipped over the notecard and on the reverse she noticed a phone number. His cell. And beneath the digits, another message.

If you need anything, call me anytime.

Anytime.

Unmasked

Contracts. Approvals. Back-to-back meetings. Yet throughout his busy work day, all Devon could think about was Angel. By 6pm that night, he couldn't wait a moment longer and he speed-walked from Fairweather Holdings Group's head office, crossing the street to his apartment building. The elevator couldn't carry him fast enough.

"Come on, come on," he urged, glancing up at the display inside the elevator. 30, 31, 32...

The doors opened and he felt his pace voluntarily quicken as he swiftly moved through the hallway to the front door of his penthouse. He opened the door and rushed through to the bedroom. He stopped. *She's probably sleeping*, he thought to himself. Gingerly, he knocked at the door. He heard her stirring and cracked open the door half an inch.

"May I come in?"

"Mmmm..." came the mumbled reply. He pushed the door wide open.

The sight before him caused him to gasp audibly. She was sat up in his bed holding the white sheets up over her chest. Her un-styled dark hair fell softly around her face, freshly washed from the shower she had right before climbing into his bed. Sunlight peaked around the edges of the thick curtains, immersing the woman before him in a bright light.

"You-you're... beautiful..." he whispered, his thoughts escaping his parted lips.

She blushed and glanced down, running a hand through her loose locks. In front of her, Devon stood fully clothed in his impeccably-styled suit. She wore only her underwear and was barely free from the drowsing effects of sleep. She felt vulnerable. Unmasked.

"I just woke up," she murmured at last.

Devon stepped forward and reached her side.

"You slept well, I hope?"

"Mmmm. It's comfortable up here. Quiet. I umm, I used the shower too, I hope that's okay."

As he sat down on the edge of the bed, she wracked her brain for the location of her discarded blood-stained clothing. She feared they were lying in a heap on the white marble of Devon's pristine bathroom floor. Her eyes widened. He misread her fear.

"My dear, it's quite alright. Please don't worry. You're welcome to make yourself at home. I want you to feel comfortable here, truly."

She looked up at him. His eyes met hers. He smiled warmly as he reached forward and tucked her hair behind her ear. "You are welcome here, Angel." The warmth of his smile prompted her to smile, too. Devon ran his hand over her cheek, his thumb grazing lightly over the soft, fleshy part of her face. The strap of her black lace bra fell from her shoulder and she let it fall. Devon's eyebrows furrowed as he noticed a mark on the exposed skin. A scar.

"What happened?"

His eyes searched hers and his concern showed in his deep blue orbs. His worry was heartfelt.

Angel shook her head. "Oh, it's nothing. One of many. I have a lot of them. You should've seen the other guy, I –"

Brushing off her attempt at a joke, Devon simply leaned forward and pressed his lips to the mark on her shoulder. His lips lingered there for a second longer than necessary, and he pulled away before it became an uncomfortably long gesture. But his eyes didn't leave the scar. Instead, he ran his hands along it. Up and down its center and around its edges. Every inch of it. Her eyes followed his digits tracing circles on her shoulder. He looked up at her and their eyes met once more.

"Nobody is going to hurt you again, Angel. I'm going to make sure of that."

She smiled warmly. Genuine. Unguarded.

She jumped, startled, as her cell phone alerted her to an incoming call. She knew the tone well. It was Frankie. Devon glanced down at the display.

"Do you need to get that?"

Angel's eyes were wide. Fear and uncertainty raced through her mind. Fear of what would happen if she didn't answer. Uncertainty of the ramifications it would have on – *whatever this is* – with Devon. She looked at him. Then reached for her cell.

Devon sat back on the bed and looked at the rich carpeting beneath his feet. He listened as the usually in-control assassin spoke with a waver in her tone.

I'm on a job tonight.

I can take contracts from you soon.

Frankie, c'mon. I told you I'll come back. You don't believe me?

The call ended.

Devon's tone was soft, yet it held an air of conviction.

"You're afraid of him."

It wasn't a question.

"I'm not afraid of anyone," came the curt response. Gone was the vulnerable woman before him. The *Angel of the Night* was back in the room.

"Angel..." He reached out and gently placed his hand on the side of her face. "You don't have to be strong for me."

Her big hazel eyes noticed his furrowed brows. He was a smart man. He knew there was more to the story.

"You and Frankie. You have a history," he said.

After a long pause, she started to explain, her strong voice shaking once more.

"Yes. W-we do. It's a long story."

"I have time."

"Okay, I – erm..." She paused. Was she really going to tell him this? It appeared so. "I started working for him when I was nineteen. I was working at The Blackbird Inn at the time. You know, the bar you came into? Anyway. I was making lousy money. As you've probably figured, most of the regulars are in crime. Long story short, I heard about a job with Cucinotta, working as his snitch. But I did something in the interview. Something I'm not proud of. Afterwards, Frankie became obsessed. He pursued me. I was so young, and I was flattered that a powerful man would be interested in me. So we dated. We were together for a couple years. During that time, I figured I needed to be in good shape if I was dating someone so dangerous. So I trained hard every day. At the same time, my job as a snitch expanded. I started interrogations. I learned how to fight, how to shoot. How to kill. After a couple years, I wanted out. Out of the relationship, out of the job. I wanted to work for myself. Frankie wouldn't let me leave. He threatened to kill me. I bargained with him, told him he couldn't run his business without me. He agreed, and he spared my life. The deal was that I would stay working for him and *only him*. And..." She looked up at the blond, gesturing towards herself and then him. "Here we are."

Devon had listened to her intently. He now

understood Angel's predicament fully. He saw that she wasn't quite the powerful, independent femme fatale he had assumed her to be. She was under the control of a very dangerous man. He had to help her.

"You want to be free of him?" he asked. Angel nodded.

"Of course I do. But it's not like I haven't tried to get rid of that son of a bitch. His security detail is ridiculous. You can't get near him. And anyway, now it's harder than ever. There are... there are other people involved. If I leave, he'll..." She could barely say the words, her eyes glassing over. "He'll hurt you, Devon. And I can't let that happen."

He pulled her into a hug. He held her tight. He didn't have it all figured out yet. But one way or another, he was freeing Angel from Frankie's clutches.

Angel pulled away from him and glanced to her right. She saw the pistol on the nightstand and it served as a reminder of her plan.

"Your gun. You can't leave it here."

"I'm sorry, I do appreciate the gift, but I have Mike and Will to protect me during the day. I decided it's best to keep it here beside my bed where it's of its highest and best use."

She shook her head. Her worry for Devon and the threats to his life manifested as anger. Suddenly, she erupted.

"You could have been kidnapped crossing the street Devon! Do you know how fucking dangerous Frankie is! His men are watching you!" she screamed as she gestured to the window, indicating the deadly men potentially lurking on the street below.

"I'm sorry Angel. You're right. I'll keep it with me in future."

"Good. Then you'll need training."

Ready, Aim, Fire

Angel removed the padlock and heavy chain from the rusted handles and opened the sliding double doors into the warehouse.

"This is... this is where you brought me," Devon recalled, walking into the familiar space. He glanced over to the meat hanger, "And that's where you –"

"Yeah it's a real trip down memory lane," Angel quipped sarcastically. "C'mon, we're here to work."

Angel had makeshift targets rigged to a pulley system, and walked to the corner of the space to pull the targets closer. They were crudely made from cardboard and displayed circles slapped on in red paint. Crude, but it worked. She retrieved two crates from the corner of the warehouse and walked back towards Devon, stacking the crates on top of one another to form a table. She told him to take his 0.45 pistol from the inside of his suit pocket and place it on top of the crates. He obliged. Angel placed her 9mm handgun next to his weapon. She picked it up and quickly removed the magazine. Just as she suspected. It wasn't even loaded. All this time, he had an unloaded gun on his nightstand. Rapidly, so as not to embarrass Devon, she inserted the empty magazine back into the gun.

"First thing's first. Safety," she started. "You're new to this, so keep the barrel pointing down range at all times. No waving it around. That's how accidents happen. I don't want you shooting me in the leg or something. Now. Place your index finger on the grip panel, then pick it up with your right hand. Like this."

Angel picked up her 9mm and demonstrated the

correct grip with her right hand. Devon followed her and picked up his pistol.

"Now wrap your left hand around your right. Place your thumb there. Okay, you got it. Keep your index finger down the barrel. Now, move it to the trigger." She noticed Devon's hands were shaking. "It's okay, it's not loaded. You're safe. I'm gonna teach you how to load it soon. First you need to know how to hold it."

She observed his grip. It was solid. His stance needed work, though.

She placed her loaded handgun down on the crate. Stepping behind him and placing her hand on his hips, she instructed, "Move your legs apart. Wider. Good." She placed her hand on his shoulders. "Keep your arms locked and strong. Like that. Move forward so your stomach touches the crates. It will help keep you steady. Now, you see those two points?" Angel pointed to the front sight and the rear sight on the weapon between his trembling hands. He nodded. "Line them up. Look down the barrel. It might be easier at first if you close one of your eyes."

Devon looked between the two points and lined up the front sight between the two points of the rear sight.

"It's umm, it's blurry. Is that right?" he asked.

"Yeah. The target should be blurry. The front sight, the part in the middle – that part should be crisp. Good. Now place it down."

She looked up at him. His mouth gaped open slightly and his eyes were darting from his gun lying on the crate, to the target and back to her at rapid speed. His mouth felt dry and a bead of sweat formed on his brow.

"Are you alright?"

"Yes," he nodded. "I'm just nervous. Forgive me."

"It's okay." She paused for a moment and observed

him closely. He was out of his comfort zone, big time. But this was for his protection. It was necessary. She continued her instructions. “Pick up the pistol again. Use your right hand. Turn it to the side. No, not the whole thing. Just turn your wrist. Good. Now, see the round button there?” She paused until she noticed him nodding. “Press that. It releases the magazine. The magazine is where the ammo lives. Place it down for a second.”

Devon placed his gun down on top of the crate once more and Angel showed him how to load the magazine with live bullets. He watched intently and his brain absorbed all of her actions. She handed the loaded magazine back to him.

“Pick up your gun and use your right hand again. Turn it to the side like you did before. Insert the magazine using your left hand.”

Devon tried, fumbled and, with hands still shaking, he couldn’t fit the magazine back inside the gun. “I-I can’t. It won’t – it won’t fit.”

“It’s okay,” she assured him, calmly placing her hand over his and inserting the magazine.

“T-thank you, Angel.” He looked up at her and smiled, his lips tight with nerves.

“You see this top panel of the pistol here? Pull it back towards you. It slides back. Pull it hard, it’s not easy. There. Good.” She took a step back and stood behind him. “Remember how to hold it? Do that for me.”

He steadied his right hand around the grip panel and wrapped his left hand around his right.

“Place your index finger down the barrel again. Don’t put it on the trigger until I say. It’s loaded now.”

His hands shifted and Angel corrected him, placing her hand on his back. “No, keep your hands where they were. You see this part here, the part you just pulled back? It's going to kick back when you shoot. So your hands have to be clear of that."

She kicked out his legs into a wider stance. "Keep your legs wide. It helps steady you. You'll need to keep your body strong, this one has a kick."

She found her place at his side and looked him up and down. She observed his stance. Double-checked his hand placement on the weapon. It was all precisely as she had instructed.

"Devon, you're doing great. Now. Are you ready?"

He nodded.

"Move your index finger over the trigger. Line up your front sight between your rear sight, just like you did before. Line it up with the middle of the target. And when you're ready. Shoot."

He swallowed hard. He shifted his feet, trying to find a comfortable position. He lined up his shot. His index finger lingered on the trigger and pulled back ever so slightly, testing the new sensation. His hands were still trembling, and it was challenging to maintain the shot he had lined up. He closed his eyes and pulled the trigger.

BANG.

"Oh my god," he gasped, placing the pistol down on the crate and leaping back as though it would explode at any moment.

"Are you okay?"

"Y-yes, yes I think so," he replied, looking up at her. "I mean, it's – it's exciting. But it frightens me."

"Welcome to my world," she grinned.

He couldn't help but think about her experience with weapons. Mere hours ago she lay in his bed without a stitch of make-up, and appeared in front of him like any other regular human being. While she cut an imposing figure in her red lipstick and black leather, underneath it all she was simply a person with fears and insecurities. Surely guns had frightened her at some stage?

"Were you afraid? When you first did this?"

"Shaking worse than you," she admitted. "But you get used to it. Ready to try again?"

He nodded. He picked up his pistol and shakily shot eight more times, emptying the magazine. He took his time and tried in vain to hit the middle of the target. He only grazed its edges. When he was done, he placed his weapon down.

"It seems I can't get it quite right," he sighed, defeated.

"You'll get it. It takes time. But you're shooting too low. When you shoot, remember the gun is going to kick back. So move with it. Otherwise it'll miss the target. Here, I'll show you."

Devon watched Angel as she hit the cardboard target with terrifying accuracy. Shot after shot after shot, her eyes never left the sight of her 9mm. She talked him through the process as she pulled the trigger. He understood. He knew what he needed to do to fix his shot. He asked if he could try again. Angel handed him the ammo and coached him through reloading the magazine. He completed the task himself with the help of her instructions. After a couple of tries, he finally inserted the magazine. He smiled at this small victory. He gripped the gun firmly and carefully lined up each shot before he pulled the trigger. His aim was a little better this time and he hit some of the inside rings of the target. Nowhere near the center where he was aiming, but he was already improving. He enjoyed the feeling of it. Such power in his hands. It excited him. Made him feel strong, confident. He placed his weapon down and looked at Angel. It was her turn.

"May I ask you a question?" he started. She nodded as she reloaded her weapon. "Forgive my intrusion, but I'm curious. How many... how many... men?"

Bang. Bang. BANG BANG BANG.

"You want to know my number? You know that's no question to ask a lady." She glanced at him and shot a seductive smile, before returning her gaze to the bullet-ridden target.

Bang. Bang. Bang.

BANG!

She reloaded. "Assuming you think of me as a lady."

"I confess my dear, I'm not sure what you are," he said with a wry smile. "But really, Angel. How many? How many men have you killed?"

"What makes you think they're all men?" she asked, looking down the barrel of her 9mm.

She fired off another round. Reload.

Devon sighed, exasperated at her inability – or unwillingness – to answer the question directly. "*Were* they all men?"

"All but one, yeah. There's more men in the business. So most of the people I capture are dudes. It's just a numbers game."

Devon nodded. He accepted the possibility that she just wasn't going to tell him.

"Fine. You want to know?" she sighed and placed her handgun on the crate. "I stopped counting at fifty."

Devon didn't say a word. He was frozen in place by her answer. *Fifty*?

"*What...*?" she asked, an amused look on her face. She shrugged, "Are you gonna *murder-slut-shame* me?"

"No, no... I just... how do you do it? Mentally, I mean? Mentally how are you able to? I'm not judging you. I'm just... as I said, I'm curious."

"I'm dead on the inside," she smirked, unsure whether or not she was joking. "Besides, the men I capture aren't exactly whiter-than-white. You were the only one who was innocent. That's why I didn't

Forbidden Kink

"We should talk about... your limits..." Angel gasped between kisses, pushing him through the door of his penthouse and locking the door behind them, all the while pulling his tailored suit jacket from his shoulders. It fell to the ground in a crumpled heap.

"I... trust you..." he responded, equally as breathless. "Besides... we've done this before..."

They reached the bedroom and Angel pulled back from him. There was a clear distinction she needed to explain. Regaining her composure, she stood in front of him, her hands on her hips.

"That was different. That was work. This is sex."

Devon quirked his brows at her revelation. "They're different?"

She sat down on the edge of the bed, her legs spread wide. Her elbows rested on the top of her leather-clad thighs. Devon stood in front of her. She told him to sit, and he sat at the top of the bed, his back resting against the headboard. She turned around to face him as she spoke.

"Look, I'm not stupid. I know my methods are a little... unconventional. I'm aware of the sexual side of it, of course. But I don't get any pleasure from it. It's just... it's effective."

"You don't get pleasure from it?"

"Nope. Well... okay, sometimes it's fun. But it doesn't get me off, if that's what you're asking."

"That's understandable. It's a technique. It works well in interrogations, I'm sure. It certainly did with me," he grinned. She returned his smile. "So... how do we do this exactly?" he asked, his arms wrapping around the headboard as he sat upright on the bed.

"I know some people in the scene. From what I've learned from them, it all has to be safe, sane and consensual. So, for example, you need to have a safe word. A safe word is a word that isn't sexual in any way, so –"

"I know what a safe word is."

"Alright. So what is it?"

Devon's eyes darted around the bedroom for inspiration. While he didn't require the dictionary definition Angel so readily shared with him, he also hadn't felt the need to use one before and so he needed to think fast. He cast his glance to the entry table beside the door. While the duo was out at target practice, his new maid had placed down a jug of chilled water with ice cubes and slices of...

"Lemon."

"Really?" Angel cocked her head. "Lemon. That's what you're going with?"

Devon shrugged and smirked at her before audaciously responding, "Unless you have a better idea, *Ms. S&M.*"

She shook her head in mocked frustration.

Devon couldn't help but grin. "Is that what it was, by the way? The book you were reading?" When she shot him a confused look, he continued. "When you captured me. You sat down and read a book. I couldn't see the cover, but now I'm assuming it was *The Joys of BDSM.*"

She cocked her head. "*Har-de-har.* I had no idea you were such a comedian." He playfully tossed a pillow in her direction and she feigned frustration once more. "Just you wait for your punishment, Devon."

The pillow went back and forth between them, and ended with Angel straddling Devon on the bed, kissing him roughly. Her hips started to grind into him and she could already sense his arousal beneath the fabric of his dress pants. Ever the tease, she pulled away from him. It was show time.

"So tell me. What is it that turns you on exactly?"

He looked up at her. "You really want to know?" She nodded. "And you won't judge me?" She assured him she wouldn't.

He took a deep breath and told her everything. He talked about the nights he pleasured himself, what he thought about when he did. How he longed to be controlled. To be dominated, humiliated. How he wanted to feel a release from his day-to-day position, one of power and decision-making. True to her word, she didn't chastise him. She listened. She confessed to Devon she hadn't done this before, an admission that shocked him. Her earlier words were absolute truth – this was sex, not work. She had never spread her BDSM wings outside of her jobs dominating and humiliating the criminal underworld of Rale during her interrogations and contract killings.

And now it was time, she decided.

Angel had remained sat on the bed as he shared his fantasies with her. She rose from the bed, mulling over his revelations. Wearing her leather jumpsuit, she oozed power and sex appeal. She walked over to the window, looking out in thought, her arms folded authoritatively. Suddenly, she pulled the curtains closed, turned around to face him and spat out the following words.

"You disgust me."

"M-my dear, I –" he stammered. "I-I was concerned this would unnerve you. This was never my intention, I know it's a little unusual, and I –"

"Shut up."

He looked up at her. He noticed the reality that she was, in fact, *not* disgusted with him. She was playing the role. His lips parted in disbelief. The fantasy he held in his mind for so long was now coming to fruition before his eyes. He cleared his throat and immediately slipped into character.

"Miss, please accept my deepest apologies," he said politely, deftly sliding off the bed and kneeling before her. "Please, allow me to demonstrate my devotion to you."

Angel watched as he placed his hands on the ground and kissed the black leather of her stiletto-heeled boots. A thrilling sight though it was, she acted nonchalant.

"You're pathetic," she spat, lifting up the toe of the high heeled boot he kissed, forcing him to look up at her. Playing the part to perfection, he wouldn't meet her eyes and he bashfully averted his gaze. It drove Angel wild and she was pleasantly surprised to realize she was feeling more and more worked up as their roleplay continued.

Ever so slowly, she walked back to the bed, perching on its edge. Deliberately, and looking directly into his eyes while emitting an aura of power and lust, she moved her legs apart.

"Take it off. Now."

"Take w-what off, I-I –" he stopped mid-sentence and looked up at her. She cocked her head. Instinctively he knew. His tie. "Y-Yes miss. Please, forgive me."

Hands shaking from adrenaline, he worked on his tie. He fumbled, his movements slower than she could bear.

"Faster."

"Yes miss."

She laughed wickedly. She leaned forward, her arms resting on her wide open thighs. She spoke with command. "You really are pathetic. Do you need help getting undressed? Shall I call one of your staff, *Mr. Fairweather sir?*"

Her tone mocked him. Was she being too cruel, she wondered? She glimpsed down at the all-too-familiar peak in his tailored dress pants, his arousal creating an uncomfortable tightness against the expensive fabric. The sight served as sufficient assurance for her to continue.

"Give it to me," she commanded, holding out her hand.

He looked up at her numbly.

"Look at you. You're dumb as well as pathetic," she spat as she snatched the neck tie from his hands. "Turn around."

He nodded and obeyed immediately, shuffling on the soft carpet of his penthouse. His back faced her. He remained on his knees. She tied his hands behind his back and made a tight prisoner cuff with the makeshift restraints. She pulled the knot tightly. Her hands firmly gripped his shoulders and she spun him around to face her.

"Pleasure me," she demanded.

"W-what? Miss, I-I can't... forgive me, I mean... I-I'm restrained, it would be terribly difficult for me. And I-I-don't know what you like, a-and –" he stammered, blushing furiously.

"Did I ask you for your life story?"

He looked at the floor and shook his head, defeated.

"Use your mouth."

He got to his feet and, hands tied behind his back, he moved his face towards her chest. He gripped his teeth around the zipper at the front of the leather jumpsuit and pulled it down. She held her hand to her chest, holding the material in place as the zip revealed her toned torso. His mouth inched further and further down until it was aligned with the waistband of her black lace panties. She shrugged her arms out of the jumpsuit, revealing her matching black lace lingerie. She slipped her panties to the side, revealing her femininity to him. He looked up at her, his eyes full with lust.

"May I have permission to touch you, miss?"

"Yes."

He leaned forward and his tongue teased at her entrance. He started slowly, pleasuring her as his mind pieced over how he would accomplish this act with his hands tied behind his back. He would have to modify his usual techniques given that his long fingers were out of commission for the time being. She leaned back on the bed, suppressing a moan and trying desperately to stay in character. He paused for a moment to ask, "Am I completing this to your satisfaction, miss?"

Arousal flooding her body, she rapidly sat upright and lowered her face down to his level. "You stop again. I'll hurt you. Understand?" He stuttered a yes and got back to work. In an embarrassingly short period of time, Angel felt the heat rise from the tips of her toes to the crown of her head as her heart rate increased. She let go of her control and came hard, her orgasm rocking through her like a freight train. Unable to remain upright, her torso fell back onto the bed and she lay down, her heart pounding so hard it felt as though it was in her throat. After a moment, she regained her composure. By this point her sub was deftly using his teeth to pull her lingerie back into position, before gripping the zip between his lips and pulling it upwards. She pulled her arms through the material of her jumpsuit and sat upright. Her fingers brushed down her high ponytail, smoothing down the stray hairs following the pleasure caused by his oral talents.

His bright blue eyes looked up at her. "Did I complete the task adequately, miss?"

She shrugged, "It was acceptable. Now. Stand up."

He obliged.

"On the bed. Lie on your stomach."

He lay down as instructed, still dressed in his crisp shirt and dress pants. She straddled him, her strong legs either side of his back, pinning down his arms. Desperate for friction, he bucked his hips against the bed. She noticed. She grabbed a fistful of his blond hair and pulled his head back.

"What are you doing? You really are filthy."

Again she wondered if she was going too far.

"Please place your hands on me, miss. Please. I'm begging you."

Apparently she was well within the lines of his kink comfort zone and she was about to feel further confirmation of this. Swinging her long legs off him, she flipped the financier over and pulled him off the bed, grabbing him by his bound wrists. Forcefully, she threw him against the wall and he sharply exhaled a breath as his back made contact with the hard surface. The assassin reached her hands down and stroked the prominent bulge in his tailor-made trousers.

"T-thank you miss. It's a great honour. T-thank you for placing your hands on me. I know I am disgusting."

She remembered her exact words in the warehouse on the night of his capture and decided she had made him wait long enough. It was show time. She placed one hand on the wall next to his head and leaned in to whisper into his ear as she continued her sweet torture.

"You *are* disgusting. You're twisted, fucked up, perverse..."

"Y-yes. Yes I am."

He moaned long and loud, and soon his breathing became laboured. He was nearing his limits.

"You make me sick," she whispered in his ear, speeding up her hand movements over the fine fabric, the only barrier between her skin and his length.

"O-oh god..." he stuttered under her ministrations. "P-please stop, I am about to..."

"About to what?" she demanded. His eyes shot up and he looked at her.

"I'm about to c-climax in my dress pants."

She sneered and leaned in, whispering, "You're a big boy, you can hold on."

She quickened the pace and he came hard, his release soaking the fabric beneath her grip.

She took a step back and observed the owner of Fairweather Holdings Group. He stood in his penthouse with his climax soaking his perfectly tailored dress pants, shocked, humiliated, and absolutely satisfied.

"T-thank you miss," he uttered after a few moments, his voice barely above a whisper. "Thank you. Thank you so very much for allowing my release."

"Devon. That's enough. We'll leave it there for tonight," she responded.

"W-what I don't u-understand, I –"

"LEMON. There, I called it."

Having ceased their role playing for the evening, she walked to the table besides his door, poured a glass of cold water and returned to his side.

"Here. You should drink this. You've probably lost

a lot of fluid through sweat. You were fully clothed the whole time."

Realizing his hands remained bound, she held it to his lips and helped him to drink the cool liquid, reminiscent of their warehouse encounter. He finished the entire glass within seconds and Angel gently instructed him to turn around. She untied his wrists. Red marks remained where the fabric had been bound tightly.

"Oh God, Devon – your wrists." He held his palms out in front of him and turned his hands over, examining both sides of his wrists. They *were* red. She was concerned now. "Did I go too far?"

"No," he answered honestly. "It was perfect. *You're* perfect."

He pressed a kiss to her forehead. She urged him to take a long shower. He agreed. As he walked into the bathroom, he stopped as a pile of black clothing on the floor caught his eye. He called out to her.

"Angel. Are they your clothes? Is that – is that *blood*?"

He walked back out into the bedroom with the bloodied garments in his hand. She looked at them, then looked down at his soiled dress pants.

"Yeah. Well, I guess we're both filthy huh?"

He laughed and closed the bathroom door.

Twenty minutes later, Devon emerged refreshed and altogether looking like a new man. She had waited outside the bathroom, ensuring she was within earshot should he need her. From her friends in the scene, she'd heard about a phenomenon affectionately dubbed 'Sub Drop', where the submissive would feel a range of vulnerable emotions following a session. She knew she had been pretty rough on him and wanted to make sure he was alright. It *was* all consensual, and Angel knew all too well how it felt when consent wasn't respected.

When the bathroom door finally opened, he found her sat on the edge of the bed dressed in his white towel robe. She beckoned him over. Instead he paused in the doorframe, dressed comfortably in his boxer shorts and a fitted grey t-shirt.

"Thank you for tonight," he smiled at her, then looked down at his feet self-consciously. "You know, I... I thought it used to feel good. When I was with those women. When they touched me, sometimes I felt... loved. It's strange, I know. But tonight I... it felt different. I felt cared for. I felt safe with you. Safe enough to do something I never would dream of doing with anyone else."

She smiled. Her mask started to slip.

"I'm glad," she responded, before a long pause. She patted the bed but noticed he seemed rooted to the spot where he stood, his back leaning against the door frame. "Devon... you should get some rest." She walked over to him and slung his arm around her shoulder, helping him walk to his bed. She placed him on the edge of it and he collapsed down onto it, clearly exhausted.

"Stay with me," he said, looking up at her with his blue eyes. "Please stay with me. I can't be alone tonight."

She nodded and sat down on the bed as he reached for her, wrapping his arms around her toned shoulders. Slowly, instinctively, she cradled him and allowed him to lean back into a horizontal position. Intentionally, he pulled her down with him.

"Lie here with me. Please, Angel."

Allowing a smile to appear on her face, she placed her body down next to him. They both lay on top of the sheets, Devon curling up and nestling his head into her chest. She ran her fingers through his still-damp hair, soothing him until he fell into a peaceful slumber. Other than quiet hums, the only words he uttered were, “You’re so beautiful...”

There are advantages to letting someone in, she thought as he drifted off to sleep.

Role Reversal

Devon sat in his bright, expansive open kitchen, located one floor below the living quarters of his penthouse. Dressed in his finest suit, he leafed through the newspaper as he held a white china teacup to his lips containing Earl Grey tea with a slice of lemon. His mind drifted to the previous night and how Angel had brought his fantasies to life. He smiled at the recent memory. When he awoke this morning, he found himself tucked under the covers in his bed. He remembered he had fallen asleep on top of them, and realized the usually ruthless killer must have moved him incredibly gently while he was sleeping. He was disappointed to discover Angel was not under the covers with him, but rather in her usual position overlooking his bed. She hadn't slept, she told him when he asked. She was standing guard, protecting him as he rested.

Devon asked her to join him for breakfast and she declined. As he thought about their exchange this morning, he sighed.

"Yes Mr. Fairweather, what may I do for you sir?" His staff member rushed up to him after hearing his dissatisfaction from across the room, where she was standing with her hands clasped obediently in front of her.

"I'm fine Frances. Really."

"Are you certain, sir? Would you like something else to eat? Some more tea, perhaps?" she urged.

"No, thank you," he responded and forced a smile. "But if you would fetch the extra breakfast items I ordered, that would be much appreciated."

She nodded and left the room.

His cell phone rang and he answered, frustrated. "What is it? For god's sake. What the hell are we paying him for then? Call him. I don't care if he's on the golf course. No, I won't make a decision on it now. Well, that's unfortunate. You will have to wait until I get to the office."

He ended the call and stood as Frances returned with a tray full of breakfast items. One of everything, just as he requested. He thanked his staff and took the tray from her hands before turning to leave the room.

"Mr. Fairweather, sir, please allow me."

"Frances, please. It's fine," he replied, his tone a little more curt than he intended. Realizing his tone, he added, "I'm very happy with your work. You needn't worry. There is simply... a change of plan today."

He left the room with the tray and returned to the level above. He opened the door and found Angel getting ready to leave. His face fell.

"You're leaving?"

"Yeah. I need to rest. I have a big job tonight."

"Well, why don't you rest here? At least have some breakfast before you go."

Her eyes perused the tray of food and she grabbed a croissant.

She grinned. "You're lucky I'm hungry."

She made her way back to the bedroom as Devon followed closely behind with the baked goods. He placed the tray down on the nightstand. She took a seat on the chaise in front of his bed, sitting with one leg bent, her heel digging into the fabric of the seat beneath her.

"Don't you have staff to do that?" she frowned as she gestured towards the breakfast spread.

"Well, yes. But I wanted to do this. For you." He

looked down at the ground self-consciously and decided to play down his gesture. "Well, I-I didn't make it myself. So it's really not much trouble."

"It's nice of you. Thank you." She smiled at him. The contented look on her face was everything he had hoped for.

"Angel, I was hoping, well I-I thought that... gosh. How do I say this," he muttered as he placed down the tray of food. "Well. I would like you to stay here. Regularly. Or, whenever you would like to, really. I know you don't need me. You owe me absolutely nothing. And I'm incredibly grateful for everything you've done for me. I suppose staying here would be my way of repaying you. Helping you."

"I don't need your help."

"Yes, I know. I'm sorry. I would like to know that you're safe. And it would mean a lot to me. If you stayed."

Angel thought about his proposal. She *didn't* need him. But that didn't mean she didn't want to spend a little more time with the man she once called her target. She decided to compromise.

"How about this. I'll go rest in my usual spot today. Then I'll come back after my job tonight. Besides, I have the keys already. From George. Oh! You should have this." She slid a key from the inside of her boot. "This is for the warehouse. You should go practise tonight. And make sure you take your guys with you for protection. Frankie knows about the warehouse. Stay safe, okay?"

His face warmed as his smile grew wide. He couldn't contain the glow that spread throughout his expression. This small gesture was Angel's way of showing she cared. He knew her well enough to be sure of this.

"A key to your place? Things are getting serious, I

see," he quipped. He couldn't help himself.

She rolled her eyes playfully. He thought for a moment that he could see her blush, but he couldn't be sure. He walked towards her and leaned down, kissing her deeply as he used his elegant hands to raise her face to his. "I look forward to seeing you tonight, Angel."

* * *

After his workday, Devon made his way to the warehouse and he felt comfortable enough to introduce one of his most trusted aides to the now-familiar space. Will stood guard as Devon let off round after round after round. Adept at maintaining a completely neutral tone, Will raised an eyebrow at his boss. He had not witnessed these skills from the usually polite and mild-mannered Mr. Fairweather, although he had suspected a change in his personality since the introduction of a certain feisty assassin. Will wasn't fully aware of what had transpired between his boss and the gun-slinger since locating her at her regular watering hole, but he correctly assumed she had become significant after he had been tasked with guarding Fairweather's penthouse while she had slept in his bed during the day. The decision left Devon with only Mike for protection, a risk Devon was more than confident taking.

Devon's instructions to his methodical bodyguard? Simply, "Protect her. At all costs."

The doors of the warehouse suddenly slid open and the financier spun towards the doors and aimed his gun at the intruder. The man raised his hands in defense and Devon immediately noticed it was the other half of his security detail. Mike.

"Woah woah woah! Stop! Devon it's me!"

Devon lowered his pistol.

"Jesus Christ," gasped Mike when he reached his boss' side.

"My apologies, Michael. You startled me."

"Yeah well you scared the shit out of me there, mate."

Following the brief altercation, Mike and Will stood back as they watched their boss continue his shooting practice. An hour passed quickly and his shots became more precise and deadly as time rolled on. The two men exchanged glances with one another. It was Mike who spoke first.

"Fuckin' hell."

"For once, we agree. What on earth is he thinking? He's a businessman, not some common thug."

"He's protecting himself. He's pretty good, too. Might work us out of a job," Mike mused.

"I have no qualms with my aim, my dear friend. Speak for yourself."

"You don't get it, do you?" Mike retorted, his voice an urgent but hushed whisper. "That mob guy Frankie, he's not fucking around. Good job one of us knows how to handle his sort."

Will remained stony-faced, his eyes fixed on his boss. He simply replied, "At least we can agree on one thing. He *is* changing. It's a shame the business is slipping from his view."

"You what?" Mike spoke louder than he intended.

"Keep your voice down, my dear comrade," Will urged before lowering his tone once more. "I overheard Charlie talking to a member of the board. There are issues. Mr. Fairweather is allowing certain details to fall through the cracks."

"Well, we need to tell him."

"Would you like to volunteer for the task?" Will

asked rhetorically.

Mike observed Devon shooting the target repeatedly. He shook his head. "You're right, mate. Let's keep schtum. He's a smart guy. He'll be alright."

The warehouse doors slid open once more and Devon's security detail aimed their handguns at the entrance. Devon barely looked up. He knew who to expect. The familiar clicking of heels on concrete only confirmed this. Without removing his eyes from his target practice, he ordered his men. "It's Angel. She's with me."

As the sound of her heels ceased their echoes around the open space, Devon looked up. Why wasn't she walking over to him? She was setting up the meat hanger, he noticed. He approached her. His security followed. She barely noticed him, too focused on her work. She held her switch blade between her teeth, cutting extra lengths of rope and laying them over the meat hanger in the event she needed them tonight. Practicality dictated she use plastic cable ties, with rope used only as a loose restraint on targets she felt certain would not escape. And yet she enjoyed the visual effect of rope. She was a real sucker for aesthetics.

"Angel. You're preparing for tonight I see," Devon started. "I don't believe you've had the chance to meet my men. This is Michael and Will."

He gestured to his security and Angel stopped for a moment, removing her knife from her mouth using her left hand, and shaking their hands with her right.

"Gentlemen. Pleasure to meet you," she purred.

She looked each of them up and down, eyeing them. She remembered them from their brief entrance into The Blackbird Inn some time ago and surveyed them with heightened intensity now. Were they trustworthy? Were they truly capable of protecting Devon? She had to know.

"If you boys are up for a little fun, follow me."

She led them both back to the target and Devon followed. She engaged the two professionals in a shooting contest, one that Angel won.

"Best of three," Will insisted after losing the first round.

The assassin agreed, and as Will fired at the target Angel watched Mike reloading his handgun. She observed his technique, and noticed the base of a tattoo as the sleeve of his shirt hitched up. Her eyes squinted. *Was that...?*

She stepped towards him and pulled the material up to inspect the ink further. Mike froze. She recognized the emblem instantly. She glanced around her and noted Will focused on shooting as Devon busied himself reloading the magazine for his pistol. They were distracted. She leaned in and whispered to the English bodyguard.

"You worked for Eddie?"

Mike nodded. She referred to famed British gangster Eddie Burnage, who formed one half of Manchester's notorious Burnage Brothers. Two of the most feared criminals across the pond, they were highly revered in organized crime circuits for their power and their somewhat ironic modus operandi – kill quickly, and never hurt civilians. They were also known for their easily recognizable logo, one their staff freely and proudly tattooed on their limbs.

Angel smiled at the former gangster. "Eddie's former weapons guy came over to work for Frankie. Years ago now. I trained under him. He taught me how to shoot."

"Seriously? Small world," Mike responded genuinely. "He was alright to you, was he?"

"Yeah. He was fair. And he hated Frankie, so we

had something in common."

Mike smiled knowingly, before glancing over his shoulder. "Look. Don't tell the boss, alright?"

"I won't. But he's smart. He'll figure it out."

Mike grinned. He knew intellect was Devon's strong suit, but he found it amusing to think the seemingly straight-laced financier could make the enormous jump to discovering that fifty per cent of his security duo held a criminal background.

Will stopped shooting momentarily and sighed at them both.

Angel's gaze returned to Mike. "What's up with him?"

"Oh, nothing. Likes it quiet when he's shooting. He's got a stick up his arse, but he's alright."

After Will missed his final shot and consequently lost the round to Angel, Mike quipped, "Best of five?"

Angel laughed. She liked the two men. They were decent, and they could shoot. Not as well as her, but not many could match her gun-wielding prowess. She was satisfied. She walked past Devon on her way back to the meat hangers and saw him reloading his pistol with great difficulty. He looked up at her.

"It's just a tad stiff. I've got it, I just –"

Angel placed her weapon into her holster and took Devon's pistol from him. In one swift movement, she released the slider and handed it back to him. He blushed. With a wink and a kiss on the cheek, she left him with two parting words before the three men exited the warehouse.

"Be good."

As Angel returned to her work, all that lingered was the strong, overpowering scent of Will's cologne.

Lives Intertwined

Many evenings during the coming weeks, Devon found himself enjoying a post-shoot beverage in The Blackbird Inn. On aesthetics alone, he looked out of place in the rugged establishment and yet he was accepted thanks to Teddy, who he had struck an unlikely but strong bond with. As he walked into the bar that evening, he cast his mind back two weeks. It was the first time he walked into the criminal drinking hole alone.

* * *

He hesitated outside the public house for longer than he could justify, the red double doors taunting him to take a step closer. *It's for Angel*, he told himself, gaining the courage to take one step closer. He pushed the doors open and stepped inside. His eyes surveyed every inch of the grimy interior. He felt a lump in his throat and he swallowed hard. His tailored jacket hanging limply over his arm and his shirt sleeves rolled up to his elbow following target practice, Devon felt his heart rate increase as he approached the bar and stood beside the imposing figure clad in a leather vest and covered in tattoos. Devon caught the eye of the barman and cleared his throat.

"I'll have a glass of Glen Dearg."

"Excuse me?" the man behind the bar asked.

"Glen Dearg, please."

"I heard you the first time, bud," he responded,

his tone gravelly.

The sound of coughing prompted Devon to whip his head around to his left to see the motorcycle enthusiast spluttering beer from his mouth through chokes of laughter. He recognized the man from the very first time he entered the bar with Mike and Will. At the time, the biker had sat next to Angel. Tonight, it was clear the man's laughter was directed at the out-of-place entrepreneur. Devon clenched and unclenched his jaw. In a business environment, the owner of Fairweather Holdings would have ordered the offender escorted from the building, but here he didn't hold the power. Instead, he placed his hands in his tailored pockets and became entranced by the sticky floor beneath him.

After an uncomfortable period of time, Teddy looked up. "Fairweather, isn't it?"

"I-it is, y-yes. Well, Devon..." he stammered and reached out his hand, introducing himself to his unlikely associate.

"Thought so. Teddy. You know Angel?"

"Yes. Yes, I do."

"Yeah. Angel says you're alright," Teddy assured him and turned to the barman. "Hey Tony, grab him a Black Horse, it's close enough. On my tab."

"That's very kind, sir. Thank you," the blond replied while searching in vain for a hook under the bar for his suit jacket. Nothing. Reluctantly, he placed his jacket on top of the grimy surface.

"Hey, loosen up would ya? It's a dive bar, not a private school. Here." Teddy pulled up the stool next to him and patted the fabric, prompting a cloud of dust to burst into the air. Devon wrinkled his nose and pursed his lips as Teddy continued talking. "Have a seat."

Tony slid the glass of cheap scotch down the bar

towards Devon. He caught it as the amber liquid sloshed against the sides of the glass and spilled over onto his crisp suit jacket.

"Oh, goodness..."

"Jeez, can't take you anywhere," Teddy joked, attempting to put his new friend at ease. The gang member reached over and cleared the liquid from the bar top with his arm and gestured to the half empty glass of scotch. "At least it's not the expensive stuff, eh? They don't serve stuff like that here. Nothing fancy. Good people though."

Devon looked around him. While he was certain his lifestyle held a stark contrast to Teddy's, he couldn't imagine to what extent the term 'good people' was open to interpretation.

"I say *good people*," Teddy started, leaning in and lowering his voice. "I mean they're straight shooters. They do what they say. Me, I'm a simple guy. And I'm a man of my word. So when I say if you hurt Angel, you're dead – I mean it. Got it?"

Devon nodded rapidly.

"Good," the older man smiled. "Tony, grab my friend another drink, would ya! And don't spill this one."

After several hours and many more glasses of Black Horse, Devon had loosened up considerably. Teddy found his new friend fascinating – like a piece of art to be observed and learned from. Like art, it was foreign to the high ranking gang member, but he could appreciate quality when he saw it. It was abundantly clear that – beneath the layers of fine Italian fabric and boarding school mannerisms – the blond was a decent human being.

"You know, I've grown rather fond of Angel. She's very... sexy..." the suited man slurred.

"C'mon, she's like a daughter to me. Don't need to

hear that shit!" the biker joked. "Nah... Angel's a good one. She acts tough. But she ain't."

"I know," Devon thought aloud. "But she's so... pretty."

"Are you trashed, or what?" Teddy laughed.

"Yes, perhaps a little," he grinned and downed the remainder of his fifth glass. He peered over at his new friend's large hands and the four capital letters tattooed on his knuckles in faded blue ink. The cheap liquor having removed all pleasantries from Devon's social conditioning, he blurted out, "What's ANNE? Is she your wife?"

He was far too intoxicated to notice the expressions fellow patrons shot him from across the bar. He asked again. Teddy's default reaction to this question was to erupt in anger, but he held back. His friend didn't mean any harm. He lowered his voice and explained, "Anne was my wife. She died. Motorcycle accident. I was driving."

"Gosh, Teddy, I'm sorry," Devon replied, suddenly sobering up at this revelation. "I know in these situations... we say '*I know how you feel.*' But I really do. Besides, I won't bore you with my story, I'm sure you've heard it."

The large man turned to him and offered a wry smile. "You know you're really up your own ass sometimes, Fairweather? Not everyone knows your life story. So go on then... tell me."

He paused and let out a long breath before responding, "Well... my parents. Umm... they were... they were killed. It was dark. December. We were in England. My Dad was driving. And we were hit by an oncoming car. They all died. I lived."

A tough man, the biker really felt for his comrade. He knocked back the remaining dregs of his beer and his eyes stayed fixed on his hands as he responded.

"I'm sorry buddy. Really. That's horrible."

"It's okay," Devon shrugged. "It's not your fault. As I said, the term '*I know how you feel*' is so hideously overused. But, truly, I'm so sorry to hear about your wife. It's incredibly difficult to articulate the feeling, but... it hurts so, so deeply. I'm very sorry, my friend."

"Thanks, bud. It's, erm... it's alright. I mean, it's *not* alright. But you get through it. That's what the drink's for, eh." Teddy gestured towards his glass.

The two glanced up at one another. Their background, vocabulary and clothing a stark contrast to one another, it was unlikely they would find a common ground. And yet they had. There was compassion and understanding between the two men. Respect. In an instant they both realized they were not so different after all. *Where else in my life have I been so judgemental*? Devon wondered. Little did he know, the biker next to him had the same thought, albeit using a completely different internal lexicon.

"Let's have one more and call it a night, eh?" Teddy suggested as his hand gestured to their empty glasses.

"Yes, one more. And I realize my money's no good here, as you said, but please do allow me to pay for this one."

The motorcyclist nodded and called out to the barman. "Hey Tony! Break out the good stuff, Rockerfella's payin'!"

Playtime

Angel strolled into Devon's kitchen, where she found him reading the newspaper and drinking his morning tea. Grasping a black bag, she tipped it upside down onto the seat beside him, the adult toys and restraints spilling over the leather upholstery and onto the parquet flooring below. He raised an eyebrow.

"What?" she quipped. "A girl's gotta shop."

"My dear," he started, his tongue finding the inside of his cheek as he closed the newspaper and placed it on the table in front of them. "You are unlike any woman I've ever encountered."

"Well, here's how I see it. I've gotta look good for the job," she smiled playfully before pointing to the clothes encasing her toned limbs. "I earn good coin. And besides, these outfits don't come for free. They're custom, not like the crap on the racks at the sex shop. I have everything made by hand – I have a guy over in Chinatown."

He leaned forward as she talked, his blue eyes bright as he listened to her. Devon had always been curious where she procured her attire – he certainly hadn't seen anything like it at the stores he frequented, and he was certain his personal tailor would have a coronary if he was to commission a similarly risqué piece. He stood and pulled her into a kiss.

"You look ravishing my dear. Please, join me for a little breakfast."

Angel was in such a good mood, she couldn't refuse. She pushed the adult toys to one side and sat down on the leather bench opposite his large accent chair. He looked good. *Really* good. Her eyes roamed over his dark grey suit, matching waistcoat, and crisp white shirt secured with his signature blue tie. He completed the look with tan dress shoes, reminiscent of their very first encounter. *The guy knows how to dress*, she mused. Angel placed her hands on the table and pushed up to raise her body towards him. The business mogul noted her head-to-toe black leather.

"You look good. Sexy," she told him.

"*Sexy*?" he repeated. Angel had never complimented him before and he relished the moment.

"Mmmm..." she leaned forward further and looked around the room. She noticed his staff member within earshot and chose to lower her voice to a whisper. "You're sexy as hell. But only because I know your secret. How you love to be tied up. Talked down to. Dominated. Humiliated. I know how you want to become unravelled in that beautiful suit of yours."

She maneuvered around the table and stood directly in front of him. She leaned down and placed her hands on the tops of his thighs, grazing his neck with her tongue. "You smell good, baby."

Gently, he framed her face with his hand. "Angel, you drive me crazy. Do you have any idea what you do to me?"

She glanced down at his dress pants. "You're leaving me in no doubt."

She kissed him deeply, her tongue finding her way into his mouth, hot and sweet from his tea. Her hands brushed along the soft material covering his thighs. He couldn't take it. "I need you upstairs. Now."

"No. Here."

Devon glanced up at his server and his face

flushed. He cleared his throat as he instructed her to leave. "Frances. Be a dear, would you. Tell my assistant my 9am is cancelled. Something... came up. It's personal. And... you're excused, also."

"Yes, sir," Frances responded and bowed her head, her subservience now mixed with a heavy dose of embarrassment. Needing no further instruction, she gladly left the breakfast room and closed the door behind her. Angel noted the two of them were alone. It was go time.

"Stand up," she ordered.

"What, I –"

"I said stand up."

Devon rose from his club chair and bowed his head to her obediently. He didn't miss a beat. "I am ever so sorry, miss," he mumbled nervously. Just how she liked it. "I have offended you. That was never my intention. Please. Please forgive me, I'm so terribly sorry."

The two of them standing now, Devon noticed this and rectified the imbalance by immediately sinking to his knees so he was physically beneath her. He sat back on his heels, further lowering himself to the floor. She pulled out the large chair he had sat in just moments earlier and took a seat. Now *she* was in control.

"Remember who owns you, my pathetic little boy," she spat, placing emphasis on the degrading words, knowing how it turned him on. Angel's mind raced with ideas of how to punish him. She looked around the room for inspiration. Thick pillar candles burned on their table. That was a good start.

"Please do accept my apologies, miss. I must make amends. What would you have me do?"

"Undress."

"W-what... I... here?" Devon looked over his

shoulder. She wasn't sure if he was deeply in character, or if he was genuinely concerned somebody would walk in. She knew they wouldn't. Nobody would dare enter Devon's living quarters without his prior say so. Either way, he was too far gone to stop now.

She watched as he unbuttoned his blazer, perfectly tailored to his lean, fit frame. His movements were painfully slow as he shrugged the jacket onto the floor. Next, his waistcoat. His hands shook as he unbuttoned the front section and removed that, too. Legs crossed and sat dominantly, she glanced at the multi-millionaire kneeling at her feet. She leaned down towards him and whispered, "Now I wonder. I wonder where you got the audacity to make me wait?"

He looked up at her with his beautiful blue eyes, wide with his perfect combination of fear, anticipation and arousal. She grabbed him by the tie and pulled him to his feet. He yelped in pain at her strength, and he coughed and struggled to catch his breath. His heart raced. She let go of his tie with a light shove, prompting his foot to step back to steady himself. "Oh, goodness..."

"What is it? Why are you whining like a little bitch?" she demanded, hands firmly planted on her hips. He immediately dropped once more to his knees, hands in prayer.

"I'm so sorry, miss. I'll be good, I promise you, I –"

"Shut up. Take it off. Now. All of it. And make it quick."

His quivering fingers worked to rapidly remove his tie, shirt and then his trousers. Navy blue boxer shorts made of the finest Italian silk remained. Angel picked up the nearby white pillared candle, pushed him further down onto his heels and forced his torso back at an angle. With zero mercy, she swiftly turned the candle upside down and the hot wax spilled onto his chest. He cried out in pain. His arousal caught her eye.

"Yes miss," he whispered after a few moments, "Yes, I deserved that. I will take my punishment."

Hesitant for a moment as she mentally pieced together her next move, she decided to pick up the leather cuffs she had purchased that morning. Using the cuffs, she secured his hands together in front of him. "Yes, you will. And you deserve it."

What did she have planned? Devon wondered. This encounter felt different to him. Spicier.

"Lie down. Over there."

Her voice remained firm but became softer in its tone. Devon nodded and made his way over to the brown leather bench, perching on its edge before laying his back down onto the cool material. Angel stood over him with her hands falling loosely at her side. She lowered her face to his and whispered in his ear, "I'm going to try some new things. If you're not comfortable, let me know. Do you remember your safe word?" He nodded. "Good. I'll build up slowly."

Devon closed his eyes and swallowed hard.

With a firm grip, she pulled his arms above his head and ran her fingertips lightly along the soft skin of his chest. Devon's eyes remained closed and he heard the clang of metal against the table that he had dined in front of just moments ago. He assumed, correctly, that Angel was moving the toys to ensure they were within arm's reach. There were additional sounds he couldn't quite place. He wasn't sure how much time had passed when he felt weight on top of him as her long legs wrapped either side of his torso and she straddled him, prompting a satisfied sigh from the man beneath her. She used a black silk blindfold and wrapped it over his eyes. She heard his erratic breathing. "Are you okay?" He nodded and gulped hard once more.

Angel reached over to her table of torture. Arranged with medical-grade precision, she had lined up a metal pinwheel, a leather flogger, a paddle, and a bowl of ice from a nearby champagne bucket.

The seconds felt like hours to Devon, who lay helpless beneath his master as he awaited her next move. He gasped as he felt a cold, slick sensation run down the center of his chest, followed by a soft tingling feeling. Angel gripped the ice cube in the palm of her hand and allowed her fingertips to graze his skin. She explored every inch of his torso, running the ice cube around the sensitive area of his nipple, down to the waistline of his silk boxer shorts. She ran it back up to his collarbone and up over his Adam's apple and along his jawline. The remains of the ice cube kissed his lips before it melted away in her hands.

Devon felt Angel's lips on his one moment later. Soft, warm and gentle. It lasted only a moment. Next, he felt a sharp pain running along the underside of his upper arm. It felt like a million tiny needles prickling him in a linear motion.

"Ah!" he yelped. He hadn't intended to speak, but the pain caught him off-guard. Angel eased the pressure on the pinwheel. He moaned. "It hurts... it hurts so perfectly, Angel." He realized his slip and waited for his partner to reprimand him for addressing her inappropriately. She didn't. Instead, she grabbed another tool.

The feeling of leather strands started at his chest. He waited patiently as she slowly dragged the flogger over his stomach. Over the waistband of his boxers. His back lifted from the bench in ecstasy as it trailed over his arousal. He ached for her. With a small flick of her wrist, Angel snapped the toy back and allowed the leather strands to hit his thigh. Devon gasped.

"Again."

She lifted her hand six inches higher and repeated the action.

"More. Harder."

With her arm pulled back, she struck him with the leather toy at full force, his moan filling the walls of the decadent room. His heart was racing. So was hers.

"Angel. Fuck me. Please."

If he could see her expression, he would know how it mirrored his own – pure, unadulterated lust and thrill.

She slipped off her leather trousers and lifted her black vest over her head, her bra displaying her ample curves. She released her hair from its bindings of her high ponytail and shook her head, the loose waves falling and framing her face.

"Please let me see you, Angel," the man beneath her requested. He had fallen out of character. So had she. She didn't care.

She reached behind his head and pulled the blindfold loose. The silky material fell onto the rich wooden flooring beneath them. His blue eyes shot up to meet hers, full with lust. She leaned forward, inhaling the fresh scent of his cologne, and she held down his arms, still bound together at the wrist.

The only sound audible in the large room was Devon's laboured breathing as the rough lace of her panties scratched against the smooth skin of his inner thigh. Reaching the very last of his reserves, he spoke.

"Please, Angel."

Keeping him waiting a moment longer would only

delay her own gratification, she figured. In one swift movement she removed her underwear and tossed her garments aside. His lips parted as he took in her naked form. Her eyes fixed on his, she lowered her body and allowed him into her. Their collective gasps reverberated around the room.

She leaned forward, placing her hands around his bound wrists, still pulled above his head. Her lips found the space where his jawline became his neck and she teased and nibbled at the soft flesh with her ruby red lips. Her hips continued their slow, sensual circular motion around him.

His eyes closed of their own accord, his senses unable to process it all. But still he wanted more.

"I need to touch you Angel. Please," he gasped.

It would have been fun to decline his request. To tease him. To assert absolute control. *And he looks so damn sexy tied up,* she thought to herself. But she so desperately craved his hands on her body and felt genuinely incapable of continuing without his fingertips exploring her every curve. In seconds the leather cuffs fell away.

His hands found her hips and she sat up, their rhythm and pace increasing at Devon's insistence. His fingers roamed up her toned stomach, lightly brushing past her breasts and working their way through her long, dark locks. She felt his fingertips on the back of her neck and it sent a tingling sensation all the way down her spine. He felt heat rising through his body and his breath became uneven. He wanted to last for her, but it was taking Herculean strength not to let go and surrender to his rapidly approaching orgasm. He considered her pleasure more important than his own and he trailed his shaking fingertips back down the front of her body and to her center, circling around the most sensitive spot. The dark haired beauty arched her back and her neck tilted backwards as she moaned. Lightheaded as he continued to pleasure her, she gave in to him and allowed her climax to race through her, the release prompting her to fall into him as he found his pleasure seconds later.

She laid her head on his chest as their pulses slowly returned to normal. He traced circles over her back as the other hand stroked her hair. Her eyes closed.

"Take all the time you need, my love," he whispered. "There's nowhere else I need to be."

Into her World

Angel pulled on her fingerless gloves and smoothed down her hair as the morning light poked through the curtains. Devon eyed her from his resting place on the side of his large bed as he straightened up his tie. His hands on his cufflinks, he spoke.

"My love, I noticed you don't wear full gloves. I'm certain you've thought over the details, but my curiosity has the better of me. Aren't you at all concerned about fingerprints?"

She shrugged. "Why would I be? I'm not registered anywhere. I don't have an address, a social insurance number or a birth certificate. Business is in cash. I use burner cells. I don't have a bank account. Even if they find my prints, they can't trace it back to a name. I pretty much don't exist."

It was true. As a child she had slipped through the cracks of the foster care system and she never stayed in one place for long. Her 'real' name, Angelica Rose, was given to her by her first foster care family. A family who cared for her, but who had to surrender young Angelica back to the authorities when she became too much to handle. There were times when Angel looked back and thought about what might have been. She had a family who loved her, once. And she lost it by her own hands. She was fully aware that where she found herself next was entirely a result of her own decisions. Her loving family carefully discussed the options with one another and felt they had no choice but to sign papers to ensure she found a family better equipped to handle the spunky pre-teen. Passed around from family to family for several years, she would eventually end up in a state-run facility as she entered her teenage years. A facility she would break free from when the streets presented an ironically safer option.

Angel had limited knowledge of her biological parents, and from what little she knew, she was grateful to be spared any further information. Her first foster family shared with her the truth of how she came into their care. Her foster father was a specialist at Rale General Hospital. He was working late one night when he heard of a newborn left at the cradle of the emergency wing. The cradle was a space created by the hospital for a mother to anonymously leave her baby if she felt she had no other choice but to give up her infant for adoption. It had a hatch accessible from the outside of the hospital, and another hatch on the inside. Angel's mother left her baby in the cradle and walked away with tears streaming down her face. Thirty seconds later, the delayed alert sounded to inform Rale General Hospital ER staff of a drop off.

The typical next steps would be to transfer the newborn to government services and find a family through traditional channels, but Angel's foster father felt particularly called to take her in. He couldn't be sure of the age of the baby, but he was certain she was less than one week old. To this day, Angel didn't know the date of her birthday.

In her present-day line of work, Angel used all of this book-passing and red tape and its resulting anonymity to her advantage.

Devon looked up at her. He knew Angel well enough to realize this wasn't an issue he should press her on further, but he couldn't help but think about his own childhood. He had grown up in a world where everyone knew his family's name. Expectations were heavy on his young shoulders. But in so many ways, the two of them were more similar than they were different. Their environments were tumultuous and void of the love they so desperately craved.

"You're working this morning I see?" he asked simply.

"Yeah. I have a target to research. He owns a bar in midtown and they'll be counting out last night's profits. So I'm heading out there early."

"My dear, you keep shifts that would rival an emergency ward doctor. May I fetch you a coffee before you leave?"

"Sure. But what makes you think I'm not an Earl-Grey-with-lemon kinda gal?" she grinned, walking up to him and smoothing down his tie.

"I'm going to say..." He rolled his eyes up in thought. "Coffee, black, one sugar."

"Close."

"No cream, no sugar? And strong?"

"You got it," she nodded as he left the room. "Wait, where are you going?"

"To make your coffee, my dear."

"Aren't you gonna call *Servant Huff-and-chuff* to do it for you?" she smiled as she lovingly mocked him.

"My love, please. I'm quite capable of making an Americano myself."

Devon promptly headed towards the large kitchen area on the floor below and spent the next twenty minutes figuring out how to use his expensive coffee machine.

* * *

After his workday wrapped up, Devon completed a

scheduled session of shooting practice followed by another visit to The Blackbird Inn. This became his new routine. He had entered a mental and emotional zone whereby everything revolved around Angel and her wellbeing, and in the process the formerly straight-laced entrepreneur had unconsciously inserted himself into her world. He spent many an evening down at the notorious drinking hole and felt immensely grateful for Teddy's friendship, meeting with him each night. But tonight was a little different.

"Romantic," Teddy quipped as he joined Devon in a secluded booth. "Why we not sat at the bar?"

"I needed to speak with you privately." He hushed his voice and glanced around the dark tavern before he continued. "About... Frankie."

"You serious?"

"Yes. I am."

Teddy knocked back his beer and glanced over his shoulder. He leaned in. "Alright. What do you need?"

"The address to his residence," Devon stated calmly.

"You ain't serious."

"I assure you my friend, I am."

"It's about Angel," Teddy stated. It wasn't a question.

"Yes. It is."

"Alright. I know a guy. Donato. Owns Lazzari's. Sicilian place on 8th. You know it?"

"Yes. I've heard the name."

"Good. Go there tomorrow. Lunch. Sit at table seven. I'll set it up with Donato."

"What do I need to do?" Devon asked with trepidation as he noticed his friend standing up.

"You'll figure it out," he responded as he left the booth. "See you at the bar in 5."

Devon remained at the booth as he thought about

the dangerous world he had involved himself in. Minutes later, he joined Teddy back at the bar as though it was business as usual.

Outside, the financial mogul's two aides waited in the town car as instructed.

Will glanced over at Mike who took his place in the driver's seat. "What on earth is Mr. Fairweather doing in there?"

"Nothin' good," replied Mike.

The following day, Devon headed out in search of the restaurant.

* * *

"Mr. Fairweather, hello," greeted the Sicilian server as Devon entered Lazarri's. He glanced at the man's name badge – Matteo. "A table by the window, yes?"

"Table seven, please," Devon requested as he cleared his throat. He was alone, having instructed his assistant to book a confidential business lunch that blocked out his calendar for the afternoon. When she asked where she should book a table, Devon was deliberately evasive and explained how the other party had booked the venue. He had to keep this private, he thought as he chewed on the end of his fingernail.

The financial mogul's discomfort waned as he sat at table seven and absorbed his surroundings. This was not some seedy back alley restaurant. It was warm and inviting, with the aroma of freshly baked pizza wafting from the open brick oven, tended to by a dark-haired man dressed in immaculate chef's whites. Devon's blue eyes scanned the menu in front of him. It appeared to be a pleasant, family-run restaurant.

"How about a plate of caprese to start?"

Devon jumped and placed his menu down onto the table as a new server appeared in front of him. Dressed in a black shirt and black dress pants, his dark hair slicked back, he stood tall in front of the blond. This man didn't look like a typical waiter.

"Y-yes, that would be lovely. Thank you," Devon stammered as he searched in vain for a name badge.

"We'll bring it right over. I'm Donato, by the way. Oh, and you should go and use the men's room. Take a right before the kitchen."

Donato's gaze lingered on Devon long enough for him to feel uncomfortable. The Sicilian restauranteur walked away and left the blond with furrowed eyebrows and pursed lips following the bizarre exchange. *Men's room?* Devon thought. *That was creepy.*

Suddenly it dawned on him. This was the next step Teddy had talked about. He removed the napkin from his lap and walked towards the restroom. Once inside, he locked the door behind him. It was a single room, with the sink in close proximity to the toilet basin itself. Devon spun from left to right, unsure of where to search first. What was he even looking for? He placed his hands gingerly on the top of the toilet cistern lid, the off-white porcelain wet beneath his grip.

"Urgh... gosh, this is revolting."

He lifted the lid and peered inside. He found nothing but stale water held within the grimy interior.

"Of course not. You're not in an old spy movie, Devon. Come on, think, think..." he mumbled to himself as he looked around the small room once more. The décor was a muddle of styles – the red brick wall stood opposite a cream painted wall. An old ceramic sink sat below a stand-alone vanity

Lifted

Angel made her way out of the emergency stairwell and stepped into the hallway of the brightly lit office space. Not a soul was visible within the glass walls of the corporate interior. But she was sure she would find him here.

Her eyes flickered to a large corner office with a man hunched over his desk, stylish pen in one hand and his other palm propped under his chin. The sleeves of his blue shirt were rolled up to his elbows with the shirt unbuttoned at the neck. His tie, suit jacket and waistcoat were hastily discarded over a guest chair in front of his desk. Large print-outs of tables and figures surrounded him.

"Devon. It's me."

He looked up at her. The dark circles under his eyes were as black as the city sky outside his floor-to-ceiling windows. He offered her a weary smile. "You're a sight for sore eyes, my love."

She was. In a black hooded jacket which concealed her bodysuit, her long legs covered in nothing but fishnets held up by suspenders, she really was a sight to behold. She also experienced an emotion that felt unusual to her but so natural at the same time – she was worried about him.

"It's midnight, baby. You should go home."

He leaned back in his large executive chair and let out a long, loud sigh. He placed his hands behind his head and arched his back as he stretched. His heavy lids closed.

"I know, my love. I know. But I can't." he sat upright and faced her. "I have an enormous amount of work to take care of."

Corporate business wasn't entirely in the assassin's wheelhouse, but she knew there *was* something she could do to make him feel better.

"Stand up."

"Angel, please. Not now."

"I said stand up."

He leaned forward, his arms crossed in front of him. "Angel, please rest assured that you are irresistible to me. But I'm afraid right now, my business needs me. Truly, I can't."

She paused for a moment, then nodded. She understood. And to Devon's surprise, she pulled up a chair and sat down in front of him, prompting curiosity and a furrowed brow from the weary entrepreneur. Her voice was soft when she asked, "Want to tell me about it?"

His expression lay blank now, drained due to exhaustion. He thought about her offer and within two heartbeats, he nodded.

"The business is suffering due to my lack of attention. It's failing. And worst of all, I realize it's failing at my hands. It's my father's company. It's my responsibility to take care of it. And it was his last wish to visit Rale right before –"

Devon's voice caught on his words and he struggled to continue. He hadn't spoke of his parents in such a long time that even the very mention of them invited a tsunami of emotions to crash over him. He felt her hand over his. He looked up at her and she smiled warmly. With glassy eyes she spoke soothingly, "It's okay. I know what it's like to grow up without a Mum and Dad."

Their eyes lingered on one another for longer than felt comfortable to the hitwoman. With a shake of her head she shrugged off the sensation and broke their gaze, casting a curious eye at the paperwork in front of him. She nodded towards the large printed sheets covering his desk.

"Mind if I take a look?"

Devon shrugged. It was worth a shot, he figured. The former lover of crime boss Frankie Cucinotta spun around the paper so that it faced her. She held out her hand and instinctively he placed his pen into it. It was heavy and engraved with his initials. A custom-made item, no doubt. She tapped the end of the pen on the side of her face as she glanced over the figures. Devon leaned forward in his seat and silently watched her over the course of around ten minutes as she scribbled lines, circles and arrows across the pages in front of her. She spun around the amended figures for Devon to read and pointed at the paper with the nib of the pen as she explained her solution.

"Liquefy your assets there. Move them here. Freeze them. Then next quarter, transfer it all into foreign money. Pounds sterling would work."

His mouth hung open. He looked down at the table of figures, up at Angel, then back at the papers again. Her proposal was not only financially sound – it was nothing short of genius-level. It was also a little unorthodox but it would absolutely work. Or in the very least, buy him some time.

"I had no idea how to... Angel, how did you...?"

"I trained under Frankie's money guy. Frankie's too stupid to handle his own finances. Anyway. I learned a lot."

"But Frankie's –"

"A criminal, yeah. But organized crime is still a business."

"Gosh, Angel, I-I don't know what to say. This is extraordinary," he gushed, picking up the papers to review the figures once more.

She grinned. "You're welcome."

Devon leaned back in his chair and closed his eyes, the relief washing over him. She had found the perfect resolution to his dilemma. Beneath his closed eyelids, he sensed a presence and opened his eyes to see her standing directly in front of him.

"Open them," she insisted as she looked down at his tailored trousers.

Devon moved his legs apart at her instructions.

"Wider."

He obliged. She placed the toe of her stiletto on his chair, resting between his legs with her foot perilously close to his manhood. He swallowed hard.

"Take off your belt," she demanded.

He immediately handed the leather strip to her. The assassin surveyed the site in front of her and realized she had made an error – the belt wouldn't work for her intended purpose. To buy her some time, she held the buckle and end of the belt in one hand and made a cracking motion with the loop. She lay the belt down on Devon's desk and reached over into her holster where she had stashed her cable ties for tonight's job. At the present moment, they would be used within an entirely different context.

Angel held the plastic ties in her mouth as she rummaged through the banker's desk drawers. She located a pair of scissors and placed them next to him. As she secured his wrists to the arms of his high-backed black leather office chair with the cable ties, she whispered in his ear, "Tell me if you want me to let you go. Deal?"

"Mmmm hmm..." he hummed numbly, his eyes closing in anticipation of what was to come.

"I need to know you're okay with this. You let me know if you're not comfortable."

He opened his eyes and his blue orbs assured her. "I will."

Satisfied with his consent, she ran her fingertips along his jawline and over his lips. Slowly, she trailed her fingers down the front of his shirt and stopped as she reached the waist of his dress pants. As she popped the button and released the zipper, Devon's eyes voluntarily fell closed. Angel kneeled down in front of him and placed her hands on his thighs. He felt his pulse increase as her hands ran up his thighs and her right hand freed his length from the confines of its fabric encasement. He was more than ready for her. She ran her tongue from the base of his shaft to the tip, swirling her tongue around the most sensitive area before she took all of him in. He exhaled a breath of pure pleasure as her soft lips moved up and down his length.

Devon shifted in his office chair. He yearned to run his hands through her long hair as she pleasured him, but the thrill of Angel's restraints turned him on immensely and would ultimately override his wish. As his head tilted back in pure bliss, he felt a sensation he hadn't anticipated – his lover's hand on his. The gesture had an intimacy about it, a closeness neither of them expected. As the assassin worked the financial mogul to his climax, her free hand rested on his thigh and her right hand stayed in its place on top of his. Slowly, so as not to startle the intimacy-averse woman, he interlaced his fingers with hers. His other hand lay on top of the arm of his chair, tightly balled into a fist.

In addition to her exceptional oral skills, Angel was respectful. Gentle, even. She didn't hurry Devon or demand he perform a demeaning task to her satisfaction. He felt safe in her hands. He trusted her. Without warning his breath hitched and his orgasm stuttered through his body.

After he reached his completion he was borderline comatose, his head tilted back and his eyes closed. Without a word she tidied him up, zipping up his crisp trousers and tucking his shirt neatly into it. Due to her diligence, no evidence of her touch was visible to the late night security officer Devon walked past later that evening, and for that he was truly grateful.

As he sat in his chair recuperating from her touch, she noticed a water cooler in the corner of his large office and returned to him with a paper cup filled with ice cold water. She placed it at his side. She reached over his guest chair to the hastily discarded suit jacket and retrieved his silk pocket square from the corner of the garment. She dabbed his now-clammy forehead with the fine material. Finally, the nearby scissors freed him from the cable ties that held him to the chair.

He regained his composure at the moment she quietly turned to leave the room. Softly, he called out to her. He asked her to stay and his deep, soulful eyes searched her face for a response. Angel declined, citing a job in the Northern Quarter.

"Allow me to walk you to the door, at least," he offered. As he did so, he searched his mind for the words to accurately articulate what had transpired within the four walls of his office.

"Thank you, Angel," he started. He felt his voice shake. "Thank you for, umm... lifting me up. I've never, well... I've never experienced this before. I've never had anyone help me in quite this way."

She smiled mischievously. Devon's gaze lingered on her for longer than necessary, relishing his last opportunity that evening to drink her in. His smile grew as she replied.

"Devon. I know I give good head, but that's taking it a little too far."

"You are funny, my dear. But I was referring to your help with the figures earlier. You didn't leave when you had every opportunity to. You stayed, and you helped me. And I've never experienced that level of help and... expertise... from a partner before. So thank you."

"Anytime, Fairweather."

With a wink and a flash of the smile he loved so much, she was gone.

The buzz of Devon's secret cell phone catapulted him back to reality. He read a sobering message from Teddy.

Donato's dead. A warning from F. Laying low for a while. You should too.

Darker

Days later, Angel found herself in her regular warehouse, completing a contract killing for a rival gang when her burner cell began to ring. She knew the identity of the caller without having to check the display. Frankie.

Angel immediately surveyed her surroundings. Where was he? She was convinced he was nearby. She ran towards the exit of the dusty space, pulling the heavy door closed behind her. The coast was clear and it seemed nobody was following her – for now. Nervously checking over her shoulder she answered the call, breathless.

"What took you so long sweet cheeks?" came his gruff voice.

"I was finishing up a job."

"A *job*, eh. Were you fucking blondie?"

"What?"

"You heard me. Blondie. Were you fucking him."

"That's none of your fucking business Frankie, and you know it," the assassin reasoned.

"Oh but it *is*, gorgeous."

His low, sinister laugh made her shudder.

"What do you want?"

"You know what I want, Ange. I want *you*. Here. Working for me. Until the day you die."

Angel fell silent as she furrowed her brows and pursed her lips – *what the hell?* It was a bizarre thing to say, even for the crime boss who was a notorious loose cannon. Her mind ticked over. *Why would he want me working for him until I'm old and decrepit? How useful am I going to be as an assassin when I'm pushing seventy?* It didn't make sense. Then it struck her. He would kill her. Soon. She knew it. Instantly, the thought knocked the wind from her lungs.

"Aaaaange..." His sing-song tone mocked her. "Don't leave me hangin', gorgeous."

The skin on her arms blistered at the reality of her situation, the hair on her arms standing on end beneath her black leather coat. Again, she glanced over her shoulder. Once more, the coast was clear. She wracked her brain, desperate to find the right words for the crime boss.

She thought back to the man she once dated. After all, she loved and cared for him once. She wasn't certain he ever truly loved her – but he did think of her fondly, once upon a time. She decided to appeal to that side of him.

"Frankie. Please listen to me. I know we've had our differences. But I still have so much respect for you. We can reach an arrangement that works for both of us. Let's talk about it, baby. Please."

In an instant he scoffed at her. She could hear his mocking through the phone.

"Nice try, Ange."

The line fell silent. She was hooped. The next words out of the mobster's mouth chilled Angel to her very core.

"You know I'm gonna kill blondie. You know that, Ange. I know you do. Question is, what are you gonna do to stop me? Wait, that's right – not a fuckin' thing. There's fuckin' nothin' you can do about it. Don't matter how many nights he spends practicing with his gun in your fuckin' warehouse."

The warehouse. *He's been watching Devon.* Angel's

footsteps ceased immediately at the realization.

She stood in the middle of the Northern Quarter with abandoned warehouses and high vantage points surrounding her. She whipped her neck to the right, then to the left, her strong body tight with adrenaline. She continued walking. She picked up her pace as she made her way towards the canal at the edge of the district. Her cell remained glued to her ear as the most gruesome details emerged from the lips of her former lover.

"You think you're so fuckin' smart don't ya, Ange. You think I'm gonna get my guys to tie up you and blondie in some warehouse and kill you both. That's too fuckin' simple. Or kidnap you and get Fairweather to pay ransom. But it ain't about the money, either. I've thought about it. Fuckin' fantasized about this shit. I'll get you both in the same place. And then I'll kill blondie. Slowly. And I'll make you watch. Then I'll let you go. You'll be on your own again. You'll be fuckin' distraught. I'll make you do whatever I want. At the end, when you're at your lowest point, *then* I'll kill you. You see Ange, I don't want to kill you. I want to fuckin' destroy you."

The call dropped as Frankie hung up the phone. Angel screamed from the very depths of her being as she hurled her cell phone into the canal in front of her.

* * *

When she reached Devon's penthouse, she was frantic. Devon wasn't there, of course. The business at risk of slipping through his fingertips, he was occupied at an emergency board meeting. Without a second thought Angel left the penthouse and raced across the street to the corporate HQ of Fairweather Holdings Group. It was 4pm, in other words broad daylight. She reached the lobby, the large, expansive corporate space a stark contrast to her head-to-toe black leather.

"Where's Devon?" she barked at the security officer on the front desk.

"Ma'am, Mr. Fairweather is currently occupied, I can –"

Angel pulled her 9mm from her holster, pointed it directly at his forehead and stated calmly, "I'll ask you one more time. Where is he?"

"Eleventh floor, boardroom, meeting, you need this –" the security guard spewed out, handing Angel a security card, his pale hands shaking.

Angel rushed to the elevator bank and found an open elevator, a group of suited men immediately displacing to make room for her. She fumbled with the security card, having never used anything like it before. Her world was padlocks and chains, not chrome elevators and security passes.

The one man remaining in the corner of the elevator nervously stepped forward. "May I?" He gestured towards the security card and Angel nodded, unsure of why the man appeared so afraid. As he swiped the pass in front of the sensor, Angel pressed floor eleven with her middle finger. Her index finger and thumb remained on her 9mm. She looked down at her weapon and placed it back in her holster. The doors closed. The air in the space was tense to say the least.

"You know Mr. Fairweather?" the man asked as he adjusted his glasses and nervously smoothed down the silk pocket square visible at the top of his blazer. His mouth hung open after he spoke, his lower lip quivering ever so slightly. Angel didn't like to scare civilians. But right now she was too focused on finding Devon to make small talk. Her morals getting the better of her, she sighed.

"Look. I'm not gonna kill you. Or Devon. Calm down."

The man nodded, seemingly satisfied with her answer.

As the doors opened onto the eleventh floor, Angel's elevator companion offered information. "You will find the boardroom at the end of the floor. Follow the hallway and turn left. Your card will grant access."

She turned back momentarily and nodded a 'Thank you'.

She swiped the sensor and opened the glass door onto floor eleven. It was bright and full of light with floor-to-ceiling glass in place of walls. The carpet was a light cream colour. The glass gave the area a blue hue. Everything about it said *Devon*. Her long strides carried her through the hallway, searching each office as she went. Each person looked up from their desk and their gaze followed her as she passed. She continued undeterred, reached the end of the hallway and made a sharp left.

The boardroom came into view. All glass. She walked along its exterior, eyeing the long table filled with sixteen executives. Devon sat at the head of the table. When his team simultaneously lost focus on him, their heads turning to the leather-clad assassin striding towards them, Devon looked up. His mouth dropped. She was *here*.

Angel reached the door and found Mike and Will.

"Boys," she said, nodding approvingly.

Mike placed a hand out in front of her as she attempted to walk past him. "Angel, look, you shouldn't go in there."

"He's in danger, Mike. Let me through."

The Manchester-born bodyguard hesitated, but after a couple moments of deliberation he stepped aside.

"Don't kill anyone, alright?" Mike urged.

Angel cast him a scornful look as she pushed the door open. Her entrance into the boardroom prompted a scream from one executive who placed her hands up in surrender. Devon noticed his dramatic board member and rolled his eyes. He was a split second away from standing up and escorting Angel out of the room. And then he looked at her. Beneath her adrenaline-fueled exterior, he saw the emotion in her eyes. Fear. He saw it as clearly as the daylight streaming through his large windows. He stood up and addressed his team, buttoning his suit jacket as he spoke.

"If you'll excuse me. I have more pressing matters to attend to."

He walked towards Angel. His eyes searched her face for assurance. He would find none.

"Are you okay?" he whispered as he reached her side.

She shook her head and her eyes filled with tears. He ran his hands up and down her arms in an attempt to soothe her. On the verge of her emotions spilling over, he slipped his arm around her waist and rushed her out of the boardroom.

"Come on, let's go home," he said reassuringly as they reached the elevator bank.

Devon's assistant rushed up to him. "Sir, forgive me, but there's a package waiting for you. It's with security downstairs. The courier won't leave until you sign for it in person. Security, they keep calling, I tried to –"

Devon sighed but assured his loyal administrator.

"It's alright. I'll pick it up on my way out."

Minutes later, the financial tycoon stumbled through the front door of his penthouse with a box under one arm and Angel slung over the other. She sat down in the foyer and Devon placed the parcel on the end table beside her. He kneeled down at her feet and held her hands in his.

"What is it, my love?"

His voice was calm. Soothing.

"Frankie. It's Frankie. I have to go back to him, Devon."

"What do you mean? What happened?"

Angel couldn't bring herself to repeat the grisly details out loud. All she needed was to protect Devon, but to do so she needed to explain the gravity of the situation to him.

"If I don't go back to him, he'll kill me. And... he'll hurt you. The warehouse, you – you need to stay away from the warehouse. He's had his men watch you and –"

Her speech rushed at a mile-a-minute and Devon couldn't make sense of it.

"Angel, slow down, please. Just explain it all. From the beginning."

Angel's eyes met the side of the brown box beside her. She stood up.

"No. No no no no no..."

"Angel, what is it?"

She pointed to the return address on the side of the package. "Frankie. That's his address."

He flipped over the box and eyed the now-familiar street address. Retrieving his keys from his pocket, he used them to break through the brown tape along its cardboard edges.

"Devon, don't! Don't open it!" she yelled, her voice hitching. She was on the verge of hysteria.

He placed a kiss on her forehead before he walked to a secluded corner of his living space. "Stay here my love. It's okay."

He pulled the tape from the box as he reached an area out of Angel's sightline. He opened it. A pungent, rotten stench released from the package. His gut informed him the contents would be grim but his intuition was unable to prepare himself for the sight before him.

A pair of severed human hands. On one hand, the words "ANNE" tattooed in faded blue ink.

Teddy.

He inhaled sharply and pressed his hand to his mouth. The packet fell to the ground.

The decaying remains of the couple's dearest friend spilled out onto the rich hardwood floor beneath him. Devon started retching. The box landed upright, displaying the plastic lining covered in the dried blood of his friend. His clasped hand was the only thing preventing him from vomiting at the horrifying reality he had uncovered.

His mind started to race. What would he tell Angel? She would be distraught. Was this *his* fault? Did Frankie know Teddy had sent him on a scavenger hunt to track down the mobster's address? *Of course he knows,* Devon rationalized. This was no accident. He held his hand to his forehead and squeezed his eyes tight shut, pressing tears to the corners of his lids. He opened them and glanced down at the blood on his hands.

This is my fault. I caused it.

Devon would be lying to himself if he said he wasn't afraid. But he was more worried for Angel than for his own safety. He knew it was a threat from Frankie. It was clear to him that the mob boss was using Angel's few loved ones as a means to keep her afraid and, ultimately, trapped and under his control.

He had to tell her the truth.

Numbly, he walked back to her side. Tears brimming over and ready to spill out onto her olive skin, she looked up at him. "Who was it?"

"It was Teddy. I'm so sorry, Angel."

He reached out to hug her and she pushed him away. She stood up and started pacing the spacious penthouse suite. *Enough,* she decided. She wouldn't accept the crime lord's reign of terror any longer. It was time for her to be free from Frankie's clutches once and for all.

"I've had enough of this shit," she snarled, heading for the door.

"Where are you going?" Devon asked after her.

"To tell that son of a bitch where he can stick his job."

"I'm coming with you," he said as he stood up, ready and willing to defend her. He checked for his silver revolver, hidden in the inside of his suit pocket.

"Devon – you're a good guy. And your shot has improved. Massively. But there's no way you can handle a man like Frankie," she said dismissively. Truthfully, she had a hunch Devon may be of some help but her stubbornness wouldn't allow her to fold and accept his assistance. Besides, he could get hurt. It was too risky.

"Angel, I can help you. I've learned so much down at the warehouse, my aim is accurate, and –"

"I said I don't need you to fight my battles, Devon!" she screamed and stormed out of the luxurious suite.

She retrieved her 9mm from its holster and ensured her switch blade remained in her knee highs.

It was time for her to take down Frankie.

Mine

Angel pulled up to Frankie's manor and walked inside the enormous property. While she entered through the imposing front doors and passed the preliminary levels of security without incident, she could feel something was off as she approached Frankie's office. This was confirmed when two of his associates stopped her. It wasn't business as usual.

"Weapons are checked at the door," one of them quipped.

"Since when?" she challenged.

A familiar voice called out from behind the double doors. Frankie.

"New policy," he said, wearing a smirk she couldn't see but could feel deep down in her gut. It sickened her.

Against her better judgement, she obeyed Frankie's order and walked through the doors to see the mobster she had grown to despise. She stood in the center of the room, arms folded and legs in a wide stance. She declined the crime lord's offer for her to take a seat. He lit his cigar and avoided eye contact with her. *This won't take long*, he thought to himself.

"Look, Frankie. Let's talk about this. Nobody else dies," she started. "I want out. I want to leave."

"I know you do," he responded, puffing his cigar and looking at her through narrowed slits. "But you're not leaving."

"Frankie, I'm sure we can come to some kind of arrangement. Come on. Be reasonable," she persuaded.

He stood up and walked towards her slowly. She felt a chill run down her arms. He looked at her, his expression still and dark. Frankie's voice was frighteningly quiet as he stated, "You're not leaving." With a jerk of his head, his goons rushed in and pinned her hands behind her back. The mob boss stroked the side of her face with the back of his hand. "Not now. Not ever. Understand? I own you, princess."

"You have no fucking idea what I'm capable of, Frankie!" she screamed as anger cursed through her. "I swear to god, if you –"

The crime lord's low laugh stopped Angel mid-sentence. He lowered his face to meet hers. "Ange, sweetheart. You have nothing on me. *Nothing.*"

With a patronising kiss on her cheek, Angel lost it. "YOU FUCKING MONSTER! I SWEAR TO GOD YOU'LL PAY FOR THIS FRANKIE –"

Frankie's goons dragged her to an adjoining room. It was an office she didn't recognize. As they dragged her, she kicked and yelled and tried to break free with every ounce of strength she had, but the three men overpowered her. Once inside the office they forced her down onto the top of the dark wood desk. They began to tear away her clothing. Layer upon layer fell to the ground as she screamed.

In an instant, the lights went out in Angel's mind. Angel didn't know exactly what had happened. She hadn't been drugged. She wasn't intoxicated. But time had started skipping on her. Vision hazy, she wasn't sure where she was. She regressed back to a place she swore she would never revisit.

* * *

"What's happening...?" she asked drowsily. "W-where

am I?"

"Shhh," the man said. "Quiet. Be a good girl now."

The man was the pastor at young Angelica's church group. She hadn't been involved in the church community previously, but one of her counsellors in the care facility where she had been placed had recommended it. Angel had attended church for two months when her pastor started actively displaying his growing interest in her. He wanted to help her be a better person, he said. She hadn't noticed the small clues he left, the seeds he had sown over the past several months to prepare her for this moment. The insults masquerading as jokes, the put-downs, all with the intention of grooming her. "God wouldn't want you to be so impure," he would say. "But of course, he would forgive you. He forgives all his children."

When he asked Angel to help set up the room before group one Sunday, she was fluttered. No, honoured. She helped out every week. It started slowly at first. Unwanted leery glances and inappropriate touches that she dismissed as an accident. After all, she had no reason to believe he had any ulterior motive.

And then it happened. That night everything went black and her world changed forever.

Angel was 14 years old when she was raped by the person she trusted the most. From that day, she swore she would never feel powerless again. And yet here she was.

* * *

"I think she likes it, Frankie!" the thug quipped.

When Angel came round from her blackout and opened her eyes to the room, she found herself on top of a desk, legs spread wide, with Frankie stood in front of her and one of his associates sat in the club chair to the side of him. The other goons were gone now. She wore only her black lace underwear, her hands tied behind her back. But in so many ways, she was naked in front of them. Fuzzy, she reached towards her shin for the switch blade she kept in her boots. She grabbed at her own skin and realized the boots had been taken from her, like so many other things they had taken so freely. Frankie laughed. "I know about the knife, sweetheart. Remember, I know all your little tricks. *I know you.*"

Angel looked down towards the side of the desk, and noticed her clothes and boots in a heap on the dirty carpet. Her knife and handgun rested on top of the leather. She had a moment of clarity. She knew what to do. But she couldn't act yet.

"You like this, huh?" Frankie said as he roughly thrust his thumb into her mouth. "Remember that day you came in for a job? I think about that day all the time. Do you think about it?"

Angel nodded, purposefully passive now. "Mmmm. I do." She moved her hands behind her back gingerly and was stunned to learn her wrists were secured with only Cucinotta's Italian silk tie. *Really?* She thought. *You have a million ways to restrain me, and you choose this? These arrogant sons of bitches think taking away my weapons is enough to stop me fighting back.* The thought filled her with power and she knew that despite her circumstances, she could outsmart her captors.

"What do you think about, Ange? Tell me." His voice was a whisper now.

"You. I think about you," she cooed. She cast her mind back to her interview one decade prior. She put herself back in that state of mind and gave him exactly what he wanted. At least for the moment. "I would like to touch you, Mr. Cucinotta. Place my hands on you. It would be an honour, sir. May I?"

Frankie hardly believed his luck and was borderline dumbstruck as he witnessed his fantasy coming to life right in front of him once again. Just as Angel planned.

He nodded and Angel started her ministrations. She took his index finger in her mouth and swirled her tongue around the outside, just like she had all those years ago. She had worked her right hand loose now and brought it forward, placing it over the mobster's digits as she eased him past her lips. He was too far gone to realize she had worked her way out of her restraints. Next, she took his middle finger in her mouth and repeated her movements.

"Oh, god... Ange..." he sighed, his head rolling back and his eyes closing. Angel noticed his relaxed posture. It was time.

She sunk her teeth deep into his middle finger and kicked him in the groin. Reaching around his back, she retrieved the handgun that rested inside the waistband of his dress pants. She tossed it out of his reach and grabbed her knife and her 9mm. As the mobster doubled over in pain, she pulled her gun at his associate and he held his hands up in defense. With Frankie still arched over, she grabbed her clothes and boots from the floor and ran.

She ran and ran and ran until her lungs burned and her throat was coarse. She made her way through the hallways of Frankie's manor, out of the front door and down the gravel driveway. Her rented town car was nowhere to be seen – they had taken it. The stones that lined the driveway dug into the soles of her feet and they bled. She didn't stop. She ran down the lane along the side of the manor, knowing she was close to reaching the main road. Hearing the sound of tires on gravel, she looked behind her. With Frankie's love of expensive sports cars, the sound of the engine was easily recognizable. The engine roared and almost growled Angel's name, taunting her.

Instantly she dived behind the hedgerow beside the lane and crouched down. She made herself as small as possible, yet her heart was pounding with fear, certain they could sense her presence. She heard the hum of the engine and saw the glow of the headlights as the black sports car roared past her and out onto the main road. She waited until the sound of the car had faded out completely, and then she waited some more. She couldn't be sure how long she hid there. But she started shivering. She realized she was huddled in a hedgerow, wearing nothing but her bra and panties, bruises already forming on her wrists. The clothes she held in her vice-like grip were now crumpled but with shaking hands she started to dress herself. "The fuck is wrong with you Angel, get it together," she spoke out loud. Soon she was clothed and as she slipped on her boots, she realized she didn't have her switch blade. Her eyes had adjusted to the dark and she looked around her tiny makeshift safe-house and noticed a glint in the dirt. "There it is. Thank god."

She glided the blade into her boot and rose to her feet. Her adrenaline now wearing off, the pain hit her fully. Her feet were cut to shreds and each step was agony. She made her way out to the main road and was thankful to notice a cab heading into the city. She jumped in.

After giving Devon's address to the driver, Angel sat back in the car, dazed. What the hell just happened? And why hadn't she taken Devon with her? *He would be no use*, she told herself. *He's not cut out for this lifestyle.* But she couldn't help but wonder. She had noticed Devon changing. He was becoming colder, more cut-throat. Ruthless.

"Not a great place for a girl to be out on her own,

is it?" the cab driver mused aloud. Angel wasn't in the mood for small talk and didn't respond. "You're asking to get attacked if you ask me."

The urge to slit his throat was immense. It crossed her mind. She let it pass. The remainder of the journey was silent.

As they pulled up outside the front entrance to Devon's building, she reached into her pocket for a $100 note. Only it wasn't there. *Shit. My cash must have fallen out when I ran.* As much as she didn't care for the attitude of her driver, she wanted to see him right and explained she would retrieve money from the apartment and come back down to him. But he wasn't going to make it so easy.

"You ain't goin' anywhere," he said as he locked the doors from the inside. "I know your type."

"My *type*?" Angel spat. Her nostrils flared and she used the rear view mirror to make eye contact with the man behind the wheel. If looks could kill, his life would have ended right there in the cab on the corner of 5th and Madison.

"Look, I don't trust ya. Gimme my money. Or you ain't goin' anywhere."

His diction mirrored Frankie's, only serving to enrage Angel further.

"Look, I *said* I would pay you," she offered, attempting to be civil one last time.

"Look, *sweetheart*, I-"

Without hesitation Angel pulled the switch blade from her boot and held it to his neck as she wrapped her arm around one side of the driver's seat. "It's inside," she stated, sinister now. "Why don't you come up with me."

Unspoken

After Angel left the suite, Devon sat in his study. He rested his hands on the fabric of the club chair and nursed his glass of scotch. He knocked it back in one shot and flung the empty glass down onto the side table next to him. He rubbed his temples. He was tired, and it was more than simply a physical tiredness. He felt exhausted with his current predicament – plainly put, he was unable to be there for Angel when she needed him. Here he was, sat in his penthouse alone when he should be helping her escape the reaches of this monster. Angel was right. He didn't possess the correct skills and know-how. He didn't have what it takes to face Frankie and take him down. What would a businessman have against a renowned criminal? All Devon had in his favour was business negotiation skills. *Perhaps I could outsmart him...* he thought to himself.

He sighed, his fatigue now affecting him physically. His eyes started to close and he pictured himself at a crossroads. He could continue the lifestyle he had maintained, or he could make a drastic change and live a life on the other side of the tracks.

Should he choose the light, or the darkness? Which one was which?

Intellectually, the right thing to do was to continue operating Fairweather Holdings Group and run the business in his family's name. But was this a sound choice given it required Devon to continue living a lie in order to maintain the charade? For so many reasons, choosing a life with an assassin didn't make any sense. But was it the obvious option if it meant Angel was safe?

His eyelids heavy, he lost track of his thought process as sleep overtook him completely.

* * *

It was a bright and clear afternoon as he walked through the park. He looked around the green, open space and noticed children with their parents. They were laughing and playing. The day was light, airy. He felt relaxed. Happy. Ahead of him he saw a young couple sat on a green tartan chequered blanket with a picnic basket. They sat under the shade of a tree, the man's back resting against the trunk as his lover rested her head on his chest. Her right hand wrapped around his lower back as the fingers of her left hand traced small, gentle circles over his stomach. Devon smiled. It was clear they were in love.

As he continued walking, he realized he knew the couple. It was his Mum and Dad. His steps quickened and soon he reached their side. Would they recognize him? They looked so young – the age of their death – and he cut a significantly different figure today compared to the 8-year-old in the back of their town car.

"M-mum? Dad...?" he whispered as he knelt down beside them. They looked at him and smiled.

"Son," Austin said softly. "It is good to see you."

Devon looked at his father, dumbfounded. Was it really a dream? Was this real?

"You look tired, Devon," his mother said, concern showing in her blue eyes. "What's troubling you?"

Devon's eyes filled with tears. He was overcome with such emotion, he could barely speak. "I have missed you both so much," he choked out. "Are you okay?"

They both smiled and nodded. His father talked next. "We are well, you needn't worry. This is where we spend our days," he said, looking up at the nature surrounding them. "But you are troubled, son. We know this."

Devon observed his father through a misty lens as his tears fogged his vision. His father urged him to speak up.

"I-I don't know how to say it. She's so like me, Dad. We seem so different, but we're the same. And we help each other. We would make a good team, I'm sure of it. But I'm scared everything is going to fall apart. I'm terrified of losing everything, absolutely petrified. Who am I to have all of this when I've done such awful things? I don't deserve to be happy."

His father stopped him and placed a hand on his son's arm. His words were kind but his tone remained firm. "Stop, Devon. You have been through enough. Of course you deserve love."

"But the business. It's suffering. And it's my fault. I'm trying to help her... and the shooting at the warehouse... but the business..."

Devon fell to his knees, the tears flowing down onto his cheeks as his head fell closer towards the ground. Isabella caught him and pulled him onto her lap. "Shhh Devon, there there. It's going to be alright. But you need to realize something, love," she whispered as she softly ran her hands through her child's hair.

* * *

The door slammed and Devon's eyes flew open, waking him up with a start. He glanced around the room and took a moment to regain his bearings. He was back in his study. He really had been dreaming.

Devon rose to his feet and noticed the empty scotch glass on the end table. He would clearly need another. Walking over to the liquor cabinet, he quickly refilled his glass and took a sip of the spicy amber liquid. He swallowed hard. He felt different. Something in him had changed. Shifted. He felt it. He knew what he needed to do next. Numbly, he walked towards the living room and called out her name.

"Angel...?"

Devon walked into his living room and, while he was taken aback by the sight in front of him, he felt somewhat undeterred given the images he had been exposed to since Angel had been part of his life. He watched as Angel, dishevelled and almost possessed with rage, beat the stranger with a solid chrome candle stick over, and over, and over. He knew her well enough to recognize this as a rage killing. Something had happened, and he needed to find out exactly what had transpired.

Devon lifted the glass of aged Scottish liquor to his lips, his other hand in the pocket of his blue dress pants, as he observed the bloodied man beneath Angel's feet.

"I am quite sure he's dead, my dear."

"IT'S NOT FUCKING RIGHT, DEVON! IT'S NOT FAIR! THIS CAN'T HAPPEN TO ME!!" she screamed at him as she stood up, gesturing erratically between her lover and the body that lay under her stiletto-heeled boots. Blood pooled from the lifeless man's mouth, staining the luxurious rug and the hardwood floor that lay beneath it.

Although blood spatter covered her olive skin and her eyes were glazed over with rage, Devon remained calm, bordering on nonchalant, as he walked up to her. The silence in the room amplified the sound of her laboured breathing, heavy from the exertion of the beating. He placed his glass down on top of the mantelpiece and slowly, purposefully, he removed the bloodied makeshift weapon from her hands and positioned it beside his scotch glass. He placed his arms reassuringly over hers. She stood there frozen, shock now showing on her beautiful face. Reluctantly she looked up at him.

"My dear, sometimes life isn't fair," he said softly. His words were too much and her emotion spilled over onto her expression. She could no longer contain all of her trauma. He held her close as the tears started to fall. "Shhh, there there," he cooed. She collapsed into him, the weight of the day now overcoming her.

"W-woah, it's okay. I've got you," Devon exhaled as he helped her to the ground. He was overwhelmed by their situation, but he held her with all of his strength. He didn't hesitate. She allowed her emotions to take her away fully and her sobs echoed around the room. The sound cut Devon like a knife, penetrating the deepest reaches of his heart. But still he held her, cradled her, and remained strong and stoic for her, as they sat in a tangled heap on the floor of his living room.

How long they stayed like that, they couldn't be sure. Devon held her until her entire being was physically drained of tears. Her sobs stuttered and eventually they became quiet hums. When he was sure she could bear it, he raised her head from his chest. Gently, he lifted her chin for her to look at him. She blinked and looked away. Placing both hands either side of her face, he kissed her. A chaste, loving kiss. No wild passion. No lust. No hint of a wild night of escapades ahead of them within the four walls of his bedroom. No. Just love.

As he pulled away from her, his fingertips caught a stray tear that leaked from her eye and rolled down her cheek. He planted a kiss where the tear had been. She looked up at him. Neither of them said a word. They didn't have to. They knew. Sometimes, the greatest meaning is taken from the words that are left unspoken.

Slowly, and ever so gently, he helped her up to standing. Her body gave way and she wrapped her now limp arms around his back.

"It's going to be okay Angel. Just trust me. You trust me, don't you?"

She nodded and murmured a quiet "Yes," as she rested her head against his chest. He gently shifted her position so her arm draped across his shoulder. He bent his elbow up so his hand could hold hers. His other hand found its place around her waist. He helped her to his bathroom.

"I'm going to run you a bath, my love. Would that be okay?"

She nodded, her mind foggy as he sat her on the side of the tub in the large, opulent marbled room. As the water filled the tub, Devon left for a moment and returned with a club chair. He positioned the chair next to the tub and carefully helped Angel into it. His suit jacket fell to the floor and he rolled up the sleeves of his light blue shirt. He removed his tie. His waistcoat remained on.

Explaining each action carefully so as not to startle her, he undressed her. Starting at her feet, he unzipped her over-the-knee black leather boots. He slipped each one off her feet. Next, he unzipped the front of her jumpsuit, looking into her eyes as he did so. Her ripped and bloodied fishnets came off next. Then her bra and panties. Bit by bit, pieces of Angel fell to the floor. She found herself completely naked in front of Devon. Naked in all possible definitions of the word.

She smiled at him. He held her gaze and smiled back. Another stray tear fell from her eye and Devon wiped it away. He slowly picked her up in his arms and lowered her into the bath.

"You're safe now, *Angelica*. You're safe now."

She melted into the hot water and for the very first time, Angelica looked up at him. Not Angel the assassin. Angelica. True, real, naked. She felt beyond safe in Devon's care. She felt cared *for.*

As he ran a sponge over her skin ever so gently, squeezing the water over her naked form, she told him everything that happened that evening. He listened. He held space for her. He looked at her with his deep, blue eyes and she felt truly heard and understood. For her sake, he ignored the anger that threatened to bubble up and overwhelm him. Those emotions could wait. Angel needed his full and undivided attention tonight, and that's what she would get.

After her bath, he wrapped her in a large white towel and helped her to bed. That night, she fell asleep in his arms.

Love Heals All

The next morning, Angel opened her eyes to the sunlight streaming through the curtains in Devon's bedroom. Something changed last night. Intuitive to a fault, she felt it in every cell of her body.

She felt something else, too. She needed someone. She needed *him*. Her mind searched in vain for the words. Instead, her actions spoke. She leaned over the bed and rummaged in Devon's nightstand, pulling out a leather flogger.

Devon sat on the edge of the bed where he had watched over her as she slept. Her actions made him furrow his brow.

"Angel, what are you doing?"

"Well, I'm... I'm doing what we always do."

Dressed in simply his boxer shorts and a white t-shirt, he slowly stood and kneeled in front of her. He removed the flogger from her hands and placed it on the nightstand beside them. He held her empty hands in his as he knelt beside the bed.

"My love. With what you endured last night, I'm afraid I can't allow us to do that."

"Devon, I need to. I need you to touch me. Please."

He looked at the fine carpet beneath his bare feet and rose to standing.

"Please, Devon," she begged, her eyes brimming with tears.

He worried his lip between his teeth for a few moments before agreeing to her request with a nod. Slowly, he climbed on top of her. Although his action was simple, he asked for confirmation. "Is this okay?" She hummed a yes. He placed his lips on hers before leaving a trail of kisses along her neck, her shoulder, her collarbone. The sensation continued down her chest all the way to her toned stomach. He rested his fingertips at her navel. And then he stopped.

"I'm sorry Angel. I... I can't."

"Please. I need –"

"You don't *need* this, you want it. The two emotions present similarly, but in actual fact they are quite different, they –"

"I don't need your psychobabble bullshit Devon, just do it!" she demanded, her nerves completely fried. But he wasn't looking at her. Still straddling her, he sat upright and his eyes became fixed on his chest of drawers.

"I know what you need."

With a sudden childlike enthusiasm, he leaped from the bed and retrieved a pair of his pajamas from the drawers. Planting a hurried kiss on Angel's forehead, he insisted, "Be back soon!" before fleeing the bedroom.

He made his way to the floor below and looked around the hallway. *It has to be here somewhere, he thought*. As he rounded the corner, he bumped into a figure. Frances.

"Mr. Fairweather sir, I am so terribly sorry for your trouble. You shouldn't have to seek me out. My apologies. Please, allow me," his hired help insisted as she scooped up the garments that had found themselves strewn across the floor following their collision.

"Gosh Frances, I apologize. Are you alright?" he asked, ensuring his clumsy act hadn't harmed her in any way. His staff member nodded and brushed down her uniform. He took the garments from her.

"Frances, would you be so kind as to show me to the laundry room please? I assume it's here on the floor?"

"Yes sir, it is. The items are delivered to you each Sunday as requested. If you have extra items now sir, I would gladly take care of it for you and deliver them to your suite."

The usually sharp business mogul was unsure how to articulate his request. His maid misinterpreted his silence and whispered, "Sir, please be assured that I will be discreet with your clothing. You needn't take care of this yourself."

He wasn't entirely certain of what she insinuated, but he shook the assumptions from his mind. "Gosh, no. It's nothing like that. I would, well... I would like them warmed up."

After an uncomfortable silence, she spoke politely.

"Yes sir. I would gladly warm up your pajamas for you. I will bring them to your suite promptly."

Frances remained poised, but her tone told him that everything he feared was in fact true.

She thinks I'm a spoiled rich kid. Or eccentric. Or both.

"No, no," he sighed, exasperated by their exchange. "I'm not explaining myself adequately. The pajamas are for, umm... my... guest."

"The lady in black, sir?" she asked right away.

"Yes. Yes, that's right. And I would like to do this for her. Would you be so kind as to show me how? And would you also have my assistant clear my calendar for the day?"

"Yes, it would be my pleasure sir." She smiled kindly now, and averted her gaze to the floor. "But perhaps I should fetch you a bathrobe, Mr. Fairweather?"

Devon glanced down at himself and realized he stood in front of his maid wearing only his t-shirt and boxer shorts. Blushing, he agreed.

Frances coached him through the workings of the industrial-sized dryer in the laundry room, for which he was grateful. He felt foolish for not knowing how to complete such a basic task, but he had simply never needed to. Despite Frances' insistence at taking care of it, he also made a cup of chamomile tea and carried it up to his suite. He tucked the warmed pajamas under his arm and held the china mug with both hands, using his elbows to press the elevator buttons and open the door into his living space.

By the time he reached Angel's bedside, only half a cup of the hot liquid remained, the rest having created a line of drops as he struggled back to the suite. Without uttering a word, his bedmate took the china cup from his hands and emptied the pool of tea from the saucer back into the cup. She smiled at him. "I learned that trick in finishing school."

He smiled, relieved. "I'm glad you have retained your sense of humour my love."

"What's up with the pajamas?" she asked.

"Oh! Yes. These are for you."

He placed her tea on the nightstand and helped her pull the nightclothes over her naked form.

"Mmmm... they're warm. It feels nice."

"Yes, it's a tradition from my mother. On cold nights in London she would place them on the radiator in our rooms. We had staff of course, but she would always do this for us before helping us into bed."

"She sounds like a good person."

"She was," he said, smiling sadly.

"She would be proud of you."

"Perhaps," Devon shrugged. "At least, I hope so."

Angel craned her neck, her eyes urgently searching the area beside the bed.

"What is it, my love?"

"My gun. Do you have it?"

"It's in the bathroom with your clothes. Would you like me to retrieve it for you?"

She nodded, insisting it would make her feel safe. He retrieved her weapon and placed it at her side along with her switchblade.

"Thank you, Devon."

He sat on the bed next to her. He searched his mind in vain, his vast vocabulary turning to dust before him. He was silent. Angel sat up in his bed, sipping chamomile tea and wearing his linens. She looked up at him.

"You don't have to treat me like an invalid, you know."

"I'm sorry. I just... I don't know what to do. I want to help you."

"You *are* helping. *This* is helping." She motioned her hand between them.

The piercing shrill of Devon's cell on the nightstand startled them both.

Devon apologized profusely and vowed to switch it off. Angel insisted he answer it. He walked into the corner of the bedroom as he did so.

Yes, that's right. Yes, I'll be out all day. I understand he's upset. I know it's important. Charlie can take the lead. Well, he'll have to. It's personal...

The words muffled together and Angel barely noticed when he ended the call and sat down on the bed beside her. Her expression was hollow. Her gaze remained on the white linen sheets beneath her as she started to speak.

"I killed him, Devon."

"Frankie? Frankie's dead?"

"No. That son of a bitch is still breathing. The other guy." She looked up at the blond, her eyes lined with emotion once again.

Devon placed his hand on her cheek. His thumb softly moved back and forth over her skin, his voice barely even a whisper. "Who did this to you...?"

Her eyes met his. She swallowed hard.

"Not last night. Another guy. Years ago, I... I was at a bible camp thing. He said he wanted me to help him, help the group. I was so young, I had no idea..."

Her voice trailed off and she stared at the back of her hands, picking at the skin around her nails.

"I remember sitting there in the group afterwards in my white Sunday school dress." She shook her head. "I just kept thinking, did it really happen? Did I imagine it? He acted as if it was the most normal thing in the world. I don't even know if he drugged me, I have no idea. My memory of it is really hazy. Anyways, I... I ran away. Lived on the streets. Then I started working at the bars for cash. And when I got the job with Frankie and learned how to shoot, I went back there. And I killed him."

Her big hazel eyes met his.

"I killed him, Devon."

"You did the right thing," he said softly. "He hurt you, Angel."

"How can you even look at me? I'm a monster." She choked on her sobs.

Without hesitation, he pulled her into a hug. He ran her long hair through his fingers as he made a vow.

"It's going to be okay, Angel. I promise you. It's going to be okay."

Slaying the Beast

"It's hardly any wonder you're tired."

"Look, unless it's urgent, I truly –"

Devon looked up from his desk to see Charlie, his Chief Financial Officer, standing in the entrance to his spacious corner office. His stature filled the door frame, blocking out the light.

"Charlie," Devon sat up straight and pulled the sides of his blazer tightly together. "What on earth do you mean?"

"Devon, please. We all know of your extracurricular activities."

Dressed in a dark navy suit, simple tie and crisp white shirt, the CFO walked towards his counterpart's desk and placed his coffee down on top of it. He stood over Devon, smoothing down his dark slicked-back hair and adjusting the designer frames of his glasses. By contrast, Devon's shirt was uncharacteristically crinkled and dark circles were evident under his eyes. Living two lives was starting to take its toll. The dark-haired man pulled up a chair and sat down in front of his counterpart.

"My personal life doesn't concern you," Devon said firmly.

"Oh but it does. When it's affecting business."

"Don't be ridiculous."

"You obviously haven't reviewed the report from Asset Services. I sent it to you last night, but clearly you were out gallivanting as per usual," Charlie deduced. He noticed Devon's blank expression and continued. "I'll summarize it for you, given you clearly haven't bothered to read so much as the executive summary. A simple read of page one would have been sufficient to alarm you. Well. I'll keep it brief. Suffice to say, we have missed an opportunity to impress our stakeholders. As a result, the $300 million investment will fall through. It will impact our quarterly report and will alarm our existing stakeholders significantly. It's likely they too will pull their investments." The CFO paused. "But as long as *she's* okay, I suppose it doesn't bother you."

Devon had never liked Charlie. His head for numbers and impressive private education allowed the blond to tolerate his long-term bean counter, but now his patience was wearing thin.

"What is she, anyway? A prostitute?" Charlie scoffed.

"No."

"She looks like one."

"Don't be ridiculous. You haven't met her, Charlie. How would you –"

"She ran into the boardroom boo-hooing during our all-day review meeting this week. A meeting we had already planned to accommodate you and your... how shall I put it... *schedule*. She waltzed in. You dropped everything and ran, and I was forced to facilitate the remainder of the session. It was incredibly embarrassing for the Board. Or have you conveniently forgotten about that?"

He remembered. It was the night Frankie assaulted Angel.

"I remember." Devon's eyes were cold as he responded to his comrade.

"What does she do exactly? Some sort of lady of the night it seems. It's evident she isn't capable of holding down a respectable job. And I'll bet she's asked you for money."

Devon inhaled through his nose slowly. Equally as drawn out, he let out a long breath through his mouth. His hands rested on his thighs as he clenched and unclenched his fists. He grinded his teeth and used every ounce of his resolve to maintain his composure.

"What school did she attend? Assuming she graduated. She looks as though she's from the streets. Can you imagine what your father would think –"

"OUT!" Devon bellowed, rising to a standing position as he slammed his palms down on his glass desk.

With a raised eyebrow, the dark-haired man walked out.

Suddenly, Devon's burner cell vibrated in his desk drawer. Already on edge, it startled him. He answered the incoming call from Mike. It was time.

* * *

The two men drove through the leafy suburb, the large trees framing the sky. What remained of the sun poked through the odd clearing in the overlapping branches. The air felt different here. Cooler.

Devon looked out of the window. "Are you sure this is right, Michael?"

Mike slammed on the brakes to avoid hitting a passing animal, prompting Devon to lurch forward in his seat and slam back with force as his seatbelt caught him. The blond used his already clammy hands to wipe the bead of sweat from his brow.

"Sorry boss. Fucking squirrel," Mike apologized as he watched the small grey rodent scamper away, its tail rolling like a wave. "Weird isn't it? That Frankie would live here. It's like fucking footballer's wives central. Look at these gafs! Massive!"

"It's a solid cover, I suppose," Devon mused. "Although I highly doubt the decision was his own. Mr. Cucinotta isn't the sharpest knife in the drawer, or so I hear."

Mike pulled the town car to a stop on the side of the quiet residential street and cut the engine. He turned to his passenger. "Boss. Look. This really isn't a good idea."

"I'm well aware of the risks," Devon replied, keeping his voice and his shoulders low to remain undetected within the protective confines of his vehicle. The financier observed his surroundings and drank in the leafy green neighbourhood, the long paved driveways and the large homes they led to. "You're absolutely certain this is Balfour Drive?"

"Yep. Checked it out last night like you told me. It's his place alright." Mike nodded his head in the direction of the crime lord's residence. "It's the one up there that looks like a fucking castle."

The property in question was enormous. While visible from the street, it was set back and protected by high hedgerows and sturdy black gates. The exterior was the shade of light cream, and its corners formed turrets. By any definition, it was a mansion.

"You sure this ain't a job for Will? I mean, why me?" the bodyguard questioned, prompting a loud sigh from his boss.

"Michael, please. There's no need to continue this charade. I'm well aware of your expertise."

Mike was consistently unflappable, however Devon noticed how his aide shifted in his seat and loosened the collar around his neck. He knew the jig was up. "Who told you?"

"Well, that depends. Who else knows about your

past?" Devon challenged, forcing Mike's hand.

"Fine," the former gang member conceded. He knew he couldn't match his boss's intellect. "She knows. Angel. Your missus."

"Angel knows of your background? How?"

"She saw my tattoo in the warehouse that day. It's, erm..." Mike lifted up the sleeve of his shirt and displayed the gang's logo. "It's the Burnage Brothers. They were pretty serious contenders on the scene in Manchester. Turns out she knew one of the guys, he ended up working for Frankie and he taught her how to shoot. She didn't tell you she knew about me?"

"No, she didn't," Devon said as his tongue lapped the inside of his cheek in thought. "Still... it doesn't matter terribly. She knew and didn't tell me. I knew, and didn't tell her. It's all awfully convoluted, isn't it."

Mike scrunched up his face, not appreciating his boss's unnecessary verbiage. "Why'd you hire me then? Why hire a gangster?"

Devon turned in his seat and looked directly at his favourite half of his security detail. "You may not think I'm what you call '*streetwise*,' Michael. But I'm not senseless. I required security after the raid and my subsequent capture. All I knew of Angel at that time was her connection to the Cucinotta crime family. I realized it was a blind spot for me, and I needed someone who understood that world inside and out. You came with a hefty recommendation from my Uncle. Besides. Do you think I hire my closest aides without researching them first?"

"You're not as green as you're cabbage-lookin', boss," Mike joked. Devon laughed – he knew the northern English slang well, and understood it simply meant he was not as 'green' as he appeared on the surface.

Time ticked by and the duo sat quietly, watching

the mobster's residence without saying another word. They would talk strategy when they reached to the safety of Devon's suite.

On the return drive to Fairweather Holdings headquarters, Mike challenged his employer.

"Look, boss. You're not gonna like this, but... you gotta learn to drive."

Sat in the passenger side, Devon cast Mike a scornful look. "You are fully aware of the reasons why I don't drive, Michael."

"I know. And what happened to your Mum and Dad, it's awful. But – what if something goes wrong?"

"What do you mean?"

"Frankie. What if his people find me and sort me out? Then you're coming out to a car with no driver. Excuse my French boss, but they would fucking gut you."

The enormity of the situation started to strike the sharp-minded business owner, and he felt a heavy sense of responsibility for the fate of his staff.

"Michael, I would never place you in any danger. I assure you of that."

"Look, that Frankie guy doesn't mess around. I know that. And I know it's risky. You're not forcing me to do any of it. But, I've gotta make sure you're alright and you can get back to Angel. Simple as that."

"Very well. Would you teach me? How to drive, I mean?"

"Course I will."

Secrets and Lies

Sat comfortably on the window seat located in the main living area of his penthouse, Devon counted cash into bundles and secured them together with money straps taken from the vault underneath Rale National Bank. His head jerked up as he heard the door click. *Was it her?* Angel told him she was out researching a target and wasn't due home for hours. The door swung open and he noticed a male figure entering his suite. He immediately drew his pistol.

"Please, don't shoot!" the figure said as he held his hands up in defence.

"Who are you? Tell me!" Devon yelled.

"I'm Sebastian, I work for Miss Angel."

"You're lying! I've never heard of you!"

"She umm, she asked me to bring you this, she said nobody would be here," he offered, handing the gunman several boxes of ammunition for the pistol currently pointed at his chest.

"Put them down. There," Devon demanded, pointing the barrel of his gun towards his mahogany end table.

Sebastian completed the task as instructed and returned to Devon. His hands remained visible to his captor. Devon maintained a steady aim, his gun pointed at the young aide, as he removed his cell from his pocket with his left hand. She picked up right away.

"Angel. It's me. Who on earth is Sebastian? Oh. And it's been him the whole time, with the bullets?

Alright. Very well."

He ended the call and looked at his target. "You're the one supplying the ammunition all this time?" Sebastian nodded, prompting Devon to lower his pistol to the ground. Slowly, carefully, he returned the weapon to its resting place in his suit pocket. "Why do you call her *miss*?"

"That's what she asks me to call her. Out of respect, sir."

"Since when? How long have you worked for her?"

"Two years, sir."

Devon thought about his next move, realizing this man was a trusted aide of his lover. He could prove useful to Devon's plan, if he executed his next actions with care and precision. He cocked his head to the side in thought. "Do you know how to drive, Sebastian?"

"Yes, sir."

"Good. I'll lead the way."

The blond walked the young criminal underling to his town car in his private garage underneath the building. He turned to his new helper, observing him through squinted eyes. He remained suspicious.

"Do you know the location of Angel's tailor?"

"Yes sir, I do. A man in Chinatown."

The two men stepped into the vehicle as Devon handed over the keys.

"Wait. No. It would be foolish to visit Angel's contact. It's best if I visit my regular... mademoiselle. I can trust you, I assume? Angel mustn't know about this."

The multi-millionaire reached into the vehicle's glove compartment and rummaged through twenty straps of $1,000 in cash. He handed five stacks to Sebastian. "Perhaps this will persuade you."

After snaking their way through the city, Devon gave his new driver instructions to find an inconspicuous location in the back alleyway to leave their vehicle. The twosome arrived at Fallowfield Tailoring and, upon entering the warm and inviting space lined with rich wooden panelling, the flirtatious millionaire elicited coos, giggles and bashful glances from the women working in the store. He was quite the regular. He found Bridgette at the front counter.

"My dear Bridgette. It's been quite some time." He eyed the woman in front of him. "I realize I don't have an appointment, but perhaps you could... fit me in?"

She caved under his smile. "Yes of course, Mr. Fairweather."

The seamstress walked the renowned entrepreneur through to a private room at the back of the store, pouring champagne into a long, crystal flute and handing it to him with a knowing smile. He thanked her and placed down the glass. This wouldn't be a repeat of his previous 'appointments' with his former lover – he needed to keep his head clear today.

"What may I do for you sir?" she asked, kneeling down in front of him and glancing up at him with her bedroom eyes. The sight caught his breath. Bridgette was beautiful.

"My dear Bridgette," he started, the waver in his voice evident. "Today I need something special from you." She smiled, and held her tape measure at the start of his ankle and worked the device up the outside of his leg all the way to his hip. She noted the measurement – it was the same number it was every time she performed this unnecessary activity. Devon cleared his throat as he felt his body responding to her touch. "Bridgette, I need you to customize a piece for me."

"Yes of course sir," she agreed. "I'll sew your initials on the inside of your cuffs. We'll use the imported fabric for the lining, as always."

She moved the tape measure to the opposite side of his ankle and ran it up the inside of his thigh, her delicate hands following. He sighed audibly and felt his arousal causing an uncomfortable tightness in the trousers personally tailored by the woman at his feet. He closed his eyes and took a moment to gather his thoughts. His brow became clammy as her gentle hands slowly reached higher and higher. His eyes shot open. *What was he doing? Angel was the reason he was here.* He swiped her hand away one moment before she touched him intimately.

"No."

She looked down at the floor, the tape measure curled up in her lap. Devon used the brief pause to tug on his suit jacket in an effort to hide the evidence of her stimulation.

"Is it me?" she said sadly. He felt awful.

"No, no it's not you my dear," he assured her. Gently, he lifted her chin and met her eyes. "You are beautiful. Please – stand for me."

She rose to her feet at his command. He took her hand and placed it on his chest. He opened the left side of his blazer and gestured to the open space. He spoke softly to her. "Would it be possible to insert a pocket here? It must be on the left side."

"Yes sir. I can do that for you," she nodded obediently.

"Thank you Bridgette. Is it also possible to add some padding to the area? So its contents are not easily detected by... security."

"Like at the airport?"

"Yes. Like the airport," Devon lied.

"I can do that. How large would you like the

pocket, sir?"

He used his thumb and forefinger to trace the size of his pistol on the inside of his suit. "Around this size." She chalked markings around his tracings. "You must be discreet about this, Bridgette. It's very important that you don't share this with anyone."

"You have my word, sir. Our time together always remains confidential," his former bedmate answered honestly.

"Thank you, my dear. I'll have my assistant collect the new piece in the coming days."

He swiftly excused himself from the uncomfortable encounter and found Sebastian guarding the door as instructed. Without a word, the two made their way to Devon's town car, parked around the rear of the building away from watchful eyes. Still wordless during the drive back to his home, his new driver parked the vehicle in the business mogul's underground parkade.

"This stays between us. Understand?"

Sebastian nodded, shutting off the vehicle and returning the keys to Devon.

"Can I help you with anything else?" Sebastian asked nervously.

"No. Go."

Devon idly made his way up to his suite and thought carefully about his next move. He didn't expect to find her when he returned home and he jumped when he noticed Angel's silhouette through the crack in his bedroom door. Her legs were spread wide as she sat on the side of his bed lacing up her thigh-high boots. She looked up.

"Please tell me you didn't kill him," she smirked as he walked into the bedroom.

"Sebastian? No. I had him drive me to... an appointment. I was simply having a new suit tailored.

That's all," he explained as he approached her.

"Why, special occasion?"

"Can't a gentleman look sharp for his lover?" He lowered his voice as he placed each hand on the soft sheets either side of her body.

"Oh, I'm your *lover* now huh?" she joked, her façade falling as she struggled to remain unaffected by his bold movements. *He never takes charge. What's got into him?* she thought.

He ran his face along her neck, inhaling her scent. His breath felt like fire against her skin. So subtle and evocative were his movements.

"I want you. Here," he whispered into her ear. His hand found its way through her long hair, cradling the back of her head gently.

Her head fell back and she sighed as he left a trail of soft kisses along her neck, shoulders and collarbone, tracing his fingertips lightly down her arm. Her skin was ablaze.

"Sadly, we will have to wait. I have work to do, my dear. Please excuse me," he whispered as he pulled away from her.

As Devon left the suite, Angel remained on the bed with her mouth falling ever so slightly open. She would show him who's boss next time, she promised herself.

She heard the door click behind him. He was gone.

Taking The Wheel

"Is Mr. Fairweather alright?" Will asked. Meticulously observant, he noted his colleague had stood guard outside the bathroom for precisely seventeen minutes.

"Yeah. He'll be alright. Just sick, that's all," Mike replied. "You still on the night shift?"

"Yes. I'm standing guard as Ms. Angel sleeps."

"Will, I know the score. You don't have to be all proper about it," Mike smirked.

At that moment, the bathroom door swung open. In front of them stood a pale, clammy-faced Devon. He wiped his mouth with the back of his hand.

"You look sick as a dog, boss," Mike quipped.

"What a tremendous observation, Michael. Now. Are you going to teach me to drive or simply stand there and insult me?"

Devon walked past the two bodyguards. Mike pulled a face at Will. "See you on the other side, mate."

The two men reached the underground parkade with Devon leading the charge.

"The keys, Michael," Devon asked.

"What?"

"Keys. I need the keys."

"I thought you had 'em. You're driving, aren't ya?"

"Must I do everything myself," Devon muttered as he walked back towards the private elevator leading directly to his floor. He returned several minutes later and handed the key fob to his aid.

"What you giving 'em to me for? You're driving."

"Yes, but – you're driving us to a quiet location

first. Aren't you?"

"Isn't this quiet enough?" Mike asked as he looked around the private parking lot. He had a point.

"Michael, if I had known your driving instruction came with a generous helping of attitude, I would have assigned the job to your co-worker."

"Hang on, boss –"

"Out of my way, please." The exasperated tycoon pushed his security guard from his position standing in front of the door on the driver's side.

"Boss, look –"

"No. I don't need your help," Devon insisted as he used his body to block Mike from accessing the door. He fumbled with the set of keys and scratched at the lock on the car door. He tried each key in turn. Nothing fit. "Why won't it work!"

"Here, I can –"

"NO!"

"Boss –"

"Michael, I said no!"

The keys slipped from his hands and fell to the floor. Devon dropped with them. He kneeled there on the ground. He looked at the keys as they lay on the concrete beneath him. He was quiet now. He felt a hand on his shoulder. Mike spoke softly.

"It's alright. It ain't easy."

Devon nodded. Slowly, he picked up his keys, stood and turned to his aid. He played with the keys in his hand and looked down at them, purposefully avoiding eye contact. Without warning, Mike pulled him into a strong hug and patted him hard on the back.

"I'm sorry, Michael. This is terribly unprofessional of me. I shouldn't have manhandled you. I do apologize."

"Don't be daft," Mike assured him.

"It's just...it's, it's... my parents..."

"I know. It's alright."

"What if – w-what if I can't do it? What if, after all this, I can't drive?"

"What if you can," Mike said simply. A man of few words, this statement was profound to Devon. What if he *could*?

"If I can, then... I can do absolutely anything. This is what I fear the most, more than anything else. More than our plan for Frankie. If I can master this, I..." Devon trailed off.

Mike pulled away from the hug and lightly tapped the tyre of the town car with the side of his shoe. "It ain't about the fuckin' car, boss. It's all up there." He pointed to Devon's temples.

He was right. This was all in his head.

As Mike turned from the car and faced his employer, he noticed how he rubbed his eyes. "Are you crying?"

"What? No," Devon lied. He swiftly changed the subject. "Umm, thank you, Mike. You know, if this vocation in security doesn't work out for you, you would make a tremendous life coach."

Mike laughed. "All it took was a bit of a tiff and a good old chin-wag for you to call me my proper name eh?" Devon couldn't stop the genuine smile that spread across his face. He trusted his aide. "C'mon cry baby... get in." Mike took the keys from Devon and pressed the button to open every door of the car. "Central locking. Fucking magical isn't it?"

Once the two men seated themselves inside the vehicle, Devon's unlikely driving instructor gave his student a run-down of the car's interior and its most important features. Devon memorized each and every detail and asked intelligent questions. He registered and stored the information in the depths of his bright mind.

"Alright, so when you're ready, pop the key in the ignition there and turn it once."

Devon performed the task with ease and looked to his aide for further direction.

"Turn it again. Now – I'll put the heating on. In the summer, this is how you work the AC, this button here," he explained. Devon looked, nodded. "Your mirrors alright? You should be able to see the car in the sides. And with this one," he pointed to the car's main interior mirror. "Make sure you can see out the back. You might have to move it. Will drove last night. He's a big lanky bastard."

Devon nodded and adjusted the mirror.

"You can laugh boss, that was a joke."

"Oh, yes. I see." Devon forced a smile and a polite laugh. "My mirrors are adjusted. What's next?"

"Start the engine."

He turned the key and heard the hum of the engine reverberate around the concrete structure. "Oh my, it's loud isn't it?"

"Yeah. Now put your right foot on the brake. No, your right foot. Keep your left over there – it's called a *dead pedal* or sommat. Remember it's not like England, there's no clutch – so your left leg is fuckin' useless. Alright, now use the gear stick here. Push that button in. Pull it back till this bit hits D. The only other stuff you need is P for park and R, reverse. Push that button in on the handbrake. Pull the stick up. Pull it up harder, it's on tight. Yeah. Let it go. Yep, all the way down. Now you can go."

"Should I signal?" Devon asked innocently.

Mike looked around the empty lot. "You're not on your fuckin' driving test."

"No, but – I'll need to take a test, won't I? To get a license?"

"Don't be soft. With your money, we can get you a

license in any name you want."

"Do you have someone who does that?"

"I can find one. Leave it to me. Anyway, stop farting around like an old woman. Drive over there." Mike pointed to an empty stall ten feet away. "Let your foot off the brake and put it on the accelerator."

"Do you mean the gas?"

"Yeah. Just get on with it."

Glancing down between his right foot and the dashboard of neon lights so foreign to him, Devon placed his foot on the pedal. His pressure was hard and the tires screeched as the car sped forward. He slammed his foot on the brake and Mike's hands hit the dashboard.

"Lucky I've got my seatbelt on. Alright, try again," Mike said.

This time, Devon successfully moved the car ten feet forward and stopped the vehicle. It was jerky, but a vast improvement on his first attempt.

"Alright. Fancy taking her out on the road?"

Devon nodded. They may as well try – after all, he had come this far. He completed a totally unnecessary mirror check and turned on his signal, only to accidentally activate the windshield wipers.

"Oh gosh, how did I –"

"Fuckin' hell," Mike sighed, unintentionally verbalising his thoughts. He knocked the wipers to the off position and told Devon to try once more.

It was going to be a very long day.

* * *

"So I talked to Angel," Mike started as he sat in the passenger side of his boss's town car. They had returned from their drive around the city with Devon behind the wheel. "There's some guy called Dino. Frankie's side kick. Seems kosher. He got Angel the interview way back when. And blow me if he doesn't fucking hate Frankie!"

"English please." Devon rolled his eyes at his friend's Manchester dialect.

"Dino. He hates Frankie. He's your in," Mike replied, his tone abrupt.

"Excellent. Now, are we able to line this up?"

"Not without letting Angel in on it, no."

"Very well. Then how will I know who this '*Dino*' is?" Devon asked.

"Well I couldn't press Angel too hard on it. But sounds like he's old-style mob. Six foot two. About eighteen stone."

Devon sighed, "I realize I'm technically British, Mike, but I barely know what that means anymore."

"I left my metric chart at home boss," his aide smirked. "Look, he's one big fucking guy. Built like a brick shit house. And he's Frankie's shadow."

Devon's mind pieced together the scenario. "So how will I know how to reach Dino once I'm inside?"

"Pray to your lucky fucking stars boss."

Obey Your Master

Devon fixed his gaze down the center of the front sight and rear sight of his pistol, pulled the trigger and hit the target with laser precision. He shot again, this time at the corner of the target. Dead on. He moved the weapon once more and shot at a new point. Accuracy again.

Each bullet hit the intended place on the target without fail. He continued shooting until the magazine became empty.

He reloaded the weapon within seconds and returned to his practice. He didn't hear the warehouse door slide open.

She watched him. His sleeves rolled up as he held the weapon with his strong stance. His tailored blazer strewn across the dusty chair, not a wrinkle visible on the charcoal grey waistcoat that matched his trousers. She walked towards him and felt her heartrate increase as she neared the man shooting with deadly accuracy.

His round emptied and he heard the clicking of her heels on the concrete flooring.

"You know you shouldn't approach a man unawares, my dear. It's not polite," he smiled flirtatiously.

"Fuck polite," she quipped.

"And pray tell me, who is this 'Polite' you speak of? Should I be jealous?"

She rolled her eyes. "You're so weird."

He took one step closer to her and whispered, barely a whisker of space between their faces, "You adore my quirks and perversions..."

Ever so softly, he ran the back of his hand along her face, the sensation sending pins and needles dancing across her skin. She wanted to give in to him. But she remembered his teasing following his recent suit fitting, a crime that had as of yet gone unpunished. She leaned in and whispered to him.

"Are you ready for some fun and games?"

Lust fogged over his expression and she had the answer she needed.

"Good. Do you mind if I kick it up a notch?"

"Please do," he insisted. Her eyes glazed over and he waited for the sweet torture that was to come.

She placed her hands firmly around his tie. "You sure you're ready?" He nodded.

Without warning she pushed him down against the cold, dirty ground. Legs sprawled and his hands flat on the concrete flooring behind him, he looked up at her like an animal caught in a trap as her long limbs made confident strides towards him.

"I am ever so sorry, miss. W-what may I offer to you as recompense?" he asked as he held his hands up submissively.

"Fucking shut up. Public schoolboy bullshit. Talk normal."

"Yes miss. I'm sorry."

"On your hands and knees like the fucking dog you are."

"On my... hands and knees?" he asked. Part of him wanted to play the role, but another side genuinely didn't believe the request.

"Are you fucking stupid? Get on your hands and knees."

He nodded and shuffled into position, she reached around his neck and roughly removed his tie. The fine fabric found its way into his mouth as Angel tied it around his face and gagged him.

"You like this don't you? You're disgusting."

He allowed his head to drop in shame. The familiar feeling in his trousers returned, a sensation the woman humiliating him so frequently elicited.

Why on earth is this turning me on? Devon thought to himself. *This is ridiculous. And yet I love it. What's wrong with me?*

He was a smart man, but he struggled to make sense of the bizarre situation he found himself in. In time he would realize the sensation of giving away control, and having someone talk so disrespectfully to him, was such a departure from his day-to-day life that it ignited a spark in him that nothing else compared to. In the immediate present, he relished every second of her degrading act.

"On your knees," she barked. He pushed off his hands and back into a kneeling position. "Now turn around. I don't want to see your disgusting face." He obliged.

"Look at you." She pointed to his arousal as she shuffled around on his knees. "Fucking disgraceful."

He nodded and bowed his head once more. His gaze averted, her hazel eyes darted around the warehouse. She maintained her strong façade, but she barely knew what to do next – her fantasy was clouding her judgement. She fetched a chair and placed it at his side.

"Sit down. Here."

He rose to his feet awkwardly and found his way to the chair. She positioned his hands around the back and bound his wrists together with rope and pulled tight. Between the bound wrists and the gag, he was fully at her mercy.

He tried to say something and the gag muffled his words.

Shit! She thought. *He can't say the safe word.*

She removed the gag immediately. She didn't want

to break character. Perhaps he was okay? She looked into his eyes, searching them. Without saying a word, he nodded. But what was he trying to say? She leaned in and whispered, "Devon, what is it?"

"I'm concerned we're not safe here. If Frankie and his men were to break in, I couldn't protect you."

She smiled at his words. She felt certain it was the other way around – *she* wanted to protect him. And yet she had left him in such a vulnerable position in an incredibly unsafe environment.

What was I thinking?

The guilt washed over her as she reached around the back of the chair and freed his wrists from their restraints. He stood up and surveyed their surroundings, eager to find a safer place for their escapades.

"Shall we go, my love? Mike is nearby, I'll have him bring the car around, he –"

She grabbed his hand firmly. The surprise of her force made him turn and face her.

"Devon. I'm sorry."

Her eyes were full of regret and she searched his face for forgiveness.

"It's quite alright my love, it's a simple mistake. I'm unharmed."

"It's not okay, Devon. It was reckless. I'm sorry."

He stepped towards her and placed one hand on her waist, softly holding her face with his other hand. His lips touched hers, ever so gently. "The only thing you need apologize for is delaying our departure to my bedroom." She let out a small laugh as he asked, "Shall we?"

The duo spent the remainder of the evening in Devon's suite, the banker happily subjected to a wide range of degrading acts within the safe confines of his home.

The Devil May Care

Dino missed having Angel around. He was fully aware of his boss's actions, and agreed with the assassin's decision to flee wholeheartedly. He also felt a deep guilt in the pit of his stomach when he thought about the night Frankie went one step into complete darkness. Dino was busy that evening managing a dispute in the entertainment district when he heard news of Frankie's attack on his former lover. He felt responsible – he should have been there.

The thought plagued his mind as he walked into Frankie's office. The mob boss had called a meeting to plan yet another dark set-up. The old-time mobster stopped in front of the crime lord, who was sat back in his club chair smoking a cigar, his head back and his legs defiantly spread.

"Talk to me Dino. What d'ya know?" Frankie mumbled, closing his eyes and allowing a plume of smoke to pillar from his rough lips.

Dino adjusted the cuffs of his crisp shirt. "You know I was thinkin', she's worth more to you alive than dead."

The crime boss snapped his head forward and opened his eyes. "You fucking joking?"

"Nah, boss," Dino replied, sitting down in the club chair opposite him. He leaned in. "I mean, she's afraid of you right?"

"Yeah. And?"

"Well, that puts you in charge."

Frankie raised his eyebrows and his eyes fell to the floor in thought. He hated to admit it, but Dino had a point.

"And besides. You loved her once," Dino started. "You had a funny way of showing it. Treated her like garbage. She loved you, though. We were pretty close, her and me. She told me a lot. I can tell ya boss, you meant a lot to her."

"That's real fucking romantic, Dino," Frankie cursed. He took a long drag of his cigar and leaned back in his chair. He sighed and his rough fingers rubbed the stubble on his chin. "She really got under my fucking skin."

He finally admitted it out loud. Ever since she pleasured him within the four walls of his office all those years ago, the tension between them was palpable. He cast his mind back to Angel's early days navigating Rale's criminal underworld. Each time she came to him with information on the rival gang member she had spied on, he would miss every word of the critical details she offered up. He couldn't focus. She distracted him. He *had* to have her. Only then would he have the ability to concentrate in her presence.

One evening he approached her, inviting her to dinner under the guise of a business meeting. Though she was cautious at first, he made her feel comfortable. Wooed her. "Look at me, like fucking Casanova over here," he had said as he handed her a single red rose. Romance wasn't Frankie's thing. But for her, the rules changed. Angel found Frankie thrilling. He was powerful and dangerous. And he wanted *her* and only her. At least at first.

Their relationship was wild and passionate. They had long, lustful encounters that would last for hours. It didn't matter where it was. Frankie's office, his table, the back-seat of his armoured car with blacked out windows. It was a lust that was impossible for either of them to contain. Frankie became intoxicated by her. But as Angel learned the inner workings of Rale's criminal underworld she became stronger, rambunctious – rebellious, even. She was unmanageable. Maintaining control over her became his sole focus until the crime lord's obsession with Angel bordered on dangerous.

And then she left him.

They could have ruled the city. The two most powerful people in Rale. He knew it. And now he was watching it all play out with someone else. He would never admit it, but he thought of her in his weaker moments. Her long black hair, her curves, those red lips...

"She's fucking dynamite in the sack Dino," Frankie quipped as he reminisced on their explosive relationship. He opened his eyes a moment too late and missed his closest confidant screwing up his face.

"Boss. Don't need to hear that."

She's like a sister to me, Dino thought. He didn't speak it aloud. He had already shown a risky amount of affection in front of the man seeking out his revenge on the assassin he had grown so fond of.

Frankie leaned forward and stubbed out his cigar. Thoughts of Angel pushed to the dark reaches of his consciousness, he was back to business.

"Tell me what you know about blondie."

His right hand man let out a sigh. While it made sense in theory, Dino swiftly realized there was no logic in appealing to Frankie's heart – it was a side of him the mobster had buried a long time ago, never to be seen again. *Now what the hell do I say to Frankie?* He had to answer the question about Devon without placing Angel in any danger. He thought on his feet and remained as vague as possible.

"Alright. Fairweather. He can shoot. But he's green. He don't know how the scene works. No idea how any of this operates." He gestured to the lair they sat in. "So umm, that's your advantage I guess."

"But that fuckin' prick knows how to shoot," Frankie spat out, obsessively stubbing out his cigar on the gold ashtray in front of him and grinding it beyond recognition. His rough fingers rubbed his chin as he leaned forward in his chair, his elbows resting on the top of his legs, still spread wide. His eyes rested on a spot on the rug covering the wooden flooring. "So what do we do now, huh?"

"That's up to you, boss."

Frankie's dark eyes remained fixed on the floor. He *had* felt deeply about Angel. He never assigned a label to their relationship but by any definition, it wasn't love. It was an obsession. He was consumed by her. Her beauty, her touch, her scent. He thought about her every minute of every day they were together. When he wasn't slamming her lean body against the nearest wall, he thought of what he would do to her. Their lust was dark, dangerous. Frankie had crossed so many boundaries with Angel he had lost count.

The day she left him, he was furious. How could she reject the most powerful and feared man in Rale? *No, it ain't going down like that*, he had thought. So he used his position to keep her under his control. She could leave him, but she couldn't walk away. She had to continue working for him or he would end her life. Simple.

And yet here he was, sitting by idly as Angel flaunted her relationship with a man she met because of an assignment handed to her by the mob boss himself. Inadvertently, with his own doing he had constructed the perfect breeding ground for their relationship to grow. He created this. His heart started pounding at the thought.

He looked up at Dino, his eyes searing with rage.

"Follow him. Follow both of 'em."

"You got it boss."

The Lion's Den

Devon watched her through the crack in their bedroom door as she dressed for the evening's contract job. She pulled on her boots, placing into the back of her right boot an object he couldn't make out. Noticing her approaching the door he stood on the other side of, he slyly slipped away. She found him looking at the skyline out of the floor-to-ceiling windows in his living space. Rale looked especially dark and sinister.

Angel walked towards him. She had noticed a change in Devon; in the past week he had oftentimes appeared lost in thought and, when challenged, he would become evasive. He was constantly in conversation with his bodyguards, leaving the room when they called for him before heading into meetings that would last for hours. She trusted him. But his behaviour was concerning to say the least.

He heard her footsteps as she approached him. Without turning around, he spoke.

"Are you training tonight my love? Or are you working?"

She stood behind him with her arms crossed as her means of self-protection. "I have a job tonight. It's a pretty simple one, some guy in the entertainment district. But it's a pain in the ass in that I'm taking him to a new place. The warehouse isn't safe anymore. Frankie knows about it."

A new place? Having planned every conceivable detail for the evening, Devon worried this would throw his scheme out of whack. He shook the thoughts from his mind and turned around to face her. He forced a smile.

"Be careful my dear," he urged.

She scrunched up her face. His behaviour was bizarre. She shrugged it off.

"Don't worry about me. I can take care of myself. See you tomorrow."

As Angel turned to leave, Devon caught a glimpse of himself in the mirror. His stomach lurched knowing he was lying to her.

"Yes. I will see you tomorrow."

His voice was absent, day-dreamy. He thought about the plan he was about to undertake. He knew the risks. He understood he may not see her tomorrow, or indeed at all. He rushed up to her with an urgency that caused her alarm.

He kissed her. Passionate and full of meaning. His strong hands on either side of her face, he breathed his emotion into her. With his lips he told her everything he wanted to say, every word he held back. She couldn't know what he was about to do. Reluctantly he pulled away from her, his blue eyes shining with emotion.

"Please know my life has been richer with you as a part of it." He lifted his hand to her face once more and gently caressed it. He placed his lips on hers softly and pulled away. "I must go, Angel. When I see you, it will be a new day."

She didn't say a word. She couldn't. She was dumbstruck. *Why was he talking like this? Was he saying goodbye?* Before she could react, he was gone.

After making two calls, Devon met Mike in the parking lot underneath his building. As he opened the car door and took a seat in the passenger side, his aide stared straight ahead, swigging back a gulp of liquor from his chrome flask. He offered it to Devon.

He waved it off.

"You sure this is the right thing to do?" Mike asked, finally turning to his boss.

"I'm sure. It's a little unorthodox, but it will keep her safe."

"She would kill you if she knew."

"I know."

"And you remember how to drive? Just in case?"

"Yes Mike. I remember. Let's go."

Mike started the car.

The journey was silent, the two men focused on the task before them. There was no need to discuss it, having spent an enormous amount of time planning it down to the smallest conceivable detail. And now hardly seemed the time to make small talk. They arrived in the designated neighbourhood. The trees lined the streets once more, only this time they blocked out the sun. It felt darker. The familiar mansion on Balfour Drive came into view.

Mike drove them up the gravel driveway and stopped the car at the front of the manor. He nodded to Devon.

"M-Michael, I – before I go in, I just want to say... I want to say thank –"

"Fuck off."

"Excuse me?"

"You heard me, boss. I said *fuck off*. Don't talk like that. I'll see you round the back."

"Y-yes Mike, of course."

The awkward exchange reaching a close, Devon exited the car and walked to the front doors of the manor. He buttoned up his suit jacket and smoothed down his pressed trousers. Watching for his entrance through the large doors, Mike pulled the car to the back of the residence as instructed.

There, he would wait.

Cucinotta's men rushed towards Devon as he entered the building. Dino waved them off.

"Leave him to me, boys."

Dino walked towards the nervous blond. "What do you want?"

"W-well, I-I – I would," Devon stammered, taking a deep breath to steady his voice. He noticed the stocky man stood before him. It *had* to be Dino. "I would like to talk with Mr. Cucinotta. About the bank raid. I believe I can help him."

Dino pulled his head back and squinted his eyes. He didn't know what to make of the man in front of him. He was out of place in Cucinotta's manor and Dino noted his shaky tone and his shoulders rising sharply with each breath. He was terrified. It reminded Dino of ten years prior when Angel came to interview for the job. Softened by the memory, he made an executive decision to let him in.

"You know you're walking into the fucking lion's den," Dino explained as he patted down Devon, checking his body for weapons before he approached the crime lord. He checked his legs and waistband. Nothing. As he edged closer to his pistol, Devon's heartrate increased. Dino moved upwards and patted down his chest.

"Y-yes. Yes, I know. He is a very dangerous man."

Should he mention Angel? Mike had mentioned Dino's loyalty to her and knew it could help his current predicament. The thought slid away as the mobster's large hands reached the outside of Devon's suit. He stopped. He looked up at the business mogul who continued staring straight ahead. The mobster looked over his shoulder. The lobby was clear. It was just them. Dino opened the financier's custom-made suit jacket and noticed the shape of the weapon. The criminal's large hands cupped the gun. He didn't need to reach into the pocket – he knew exactly what it was.

Devon froze. His heart was pounding. His eyes met Dino's. His hands shook. He was certain he would vomit. He swallowed down on the sensation.

Before he could compute another panic-stricken thought, Dino closed Devon's jacket. He leaned down to him and whispered, "Angel's very special to me. You better not hurt her. Deal?"

Devon nodded in agreement.

"You're all clear. I'll walk you in."

Devon had no idea why he had been waved through a security check given the obvious discovery of the concealed weapon. Yes, Dino was an ally of Angel's, but Devon certainly hadn't expected to be given the green light to approach Cucinotta with a loaded gun.

Frankie has clearly made some enemies over the years, he thought to himself.

Dino led them towards Frankie's lair at the back of the building, Devon following closely behind.

Every corner they turned dripped with money. Not wealth. *Money*. The air was dank, musty. Devon could smell something metallic; he rationalized that it must be dried blood soaking the pores of the walls. How many deaths the house had seen, he couldn't bring himself to calculate.

He walked down the hallways, noting the gaudy red carpet and the unnecessary gold trim that lined the edge of the furniture. It was flamboyant but it lacked refinement and elegance. Devon's interior design character assessment distracted him for a moment from the plan he was set to execute. It was as though his brain short-circuited to prevent him from fully comprehending the severity of the situation.

Turning one final corner, they stopped in front of

a large double door with heavy gold handles.

"He's in here," Dino stated flatly. He knocked on the door rhythmically, surely a secret code of sorts, Devon assumed correctly.

"Whadd'ya want?" came a gruff reply from the inside. Dino pushed the door open and poked his head through.

"Someone to see you, boss. I checked him. He's clear."

Dino turned to Devon and lowered his voice. "He's all yours. Be careful."

Devon's heart beat fiercely as he pushed the heavy door open and walked in to face the kingpin.

As the financier stepped into the room, he saw him. He was everything he had assumed and looked exactly as he had pictured. He had read him correctly from the information fed through Mike and Angel. This boded well for his plan.

Frankie didn't look up immediately. He never did. That's what he had security for. He took his time in lighting a fresh cigar before he cast his dark eyes towards his guest. He furrowed his eyebrows when he saw him.

"Fairweather?" he said, standing up and taking a fresh puff of his cigar. "Well what a fucking lovely surprise!"

Frankie's two goons drew their weapons and the mob boss waved them off.

"He's no threat."

He dismissed his men and they walked out, closing the door behind them. It was just Frankie and Devon. The business mogul cleared his throat and drew on his inner reserves of strength.

"I came to talk to you, Mr. Cucinotta. About the raid. I want to help you find out who was responsible. After all, it's hurting business for both of us."

"And what makes you think I'm gonna listen to ya, blondie? You and Ange are together. I'm not fuckin' stupid," Frankie spat out, his tone rich with envy.

The dark curtain fell. Devon should have been nervous now. That time had passed. Confidently, he waved his hand and cocked his head. "No. She thinks we are. The truth is, Mr. Cucinotta – I'm using her to get what I want."

The mob moss screwed up his face at the comment and sat down in his club chair. He leaned back, his arms bent up with his hands resting powerfully behind his head.

"Wait a fuckin' minute. You're tellin' me, all this time you've been fuckin' with her? Acting like you're Bonnie and fuckin' Clyde? And it's a fuckin' act?"

A slow smile formed on Devon's face as he looked into the dark eyes of the crime lord.

"Huh," came Frankie's response moments later. He reached forward and knocked back his glass of rye, lifting a finger from the glass to point at the financier. "You are full of fuckin' surprises, Fairweather."

"Please, call me Devon," he offered, before pointing to the spare club chair in front of Frankie. "May I?"

Noticing Frankie's nod of approval, Devon sat down opposite him. He sat upright in his chair, his hands folded in front of him. He wasn't yet completely at ease in the mobster's presence. Frankie walked towards the liquor cabinet in the corner of the room, filling his glass with rye and pouring an additional glass for his guest.

"You know Fairweather, I had you down as a pussy, but you're my kinda guy!" He reached his new friend's side and placed down the beverage.

"Devon, please. You really must call me Devon."

"Frankie." The mob boss placed his cigar in his

mouth and held out his free hand and they shook. "Fucking bitches eh. Nothing but a fuckin' ball ache."

"Yes, indeed," Devon smirked as he clinked glasses with the mobster, the two cordial now.

"Look, forget about the raid," Frankie said dismissively as he took to his seat and stubbed out his cigar in the gaudy ashtray in front of him. "It don't matter. I paid off the cops a long time ago so I'm in the clear now. Hurt you more than it hurt me, anyway. You lost a shit tonne of cash."

"Yes, it certainly impacted our bottom line. Still. Business is business," Devon waffled, piecing together the steps to smoothly transition into his scheme. He knew the mob boss didn't require help in finding the culprit of the raid; this was simply a cover to gain access to him and start a dialogue. He planned to appeal to a more personal issue. He continued talking. "You know, you and I, Frankie, we're not so different. And I can't help feeling we should... collaborate. Imagine what we could accomplish if we joined forces. We're widely considered two of the most powerful and influential men in the city, albeit from different sides of the tracks. Besides, nobody would suspect it."

Frankie listened intently. He was intrigued. "Go on."

"There is just one problem we need to... eradicate."

"Ange?"

"Yes. I took the liberty of reviewing some options. Would you care to hear them?" Frankie nodded. "The most sensible move is to trap her. Capture her, if you will. And then we could do... well. Whatever we want. You first, of course." Devon's blue eyes bore into the crime lord, the darkness glazing over, his eyes now a deep pool of ill intent. "That would solve all of your problems, I assume?"

"It would help, yeah," Frankie quipped, before cocking his head in thought. "What's in it for you?"

"Well, I confess, I've always had a dark side. I've fought it for most of my life. Meeting Angel, it... it unleashed something within me. Something I had kept inside for a terribly long time. I'm sure that sounds rather strange." Devon shook his head as he revealed the truth.

"Nah. I get it," Frankie responded and nodded his head in agreement. "That's why you've been shooting down at the warehouse then?"

"Yes. And besides, I can't assist the most feared man in Rale without a little weaponry, can I?" Devon leaned forward and grinned.

"Pretty good shot, from what I've heard," Frankie remarked. His men had been following Devon for some time, and despite his threats to Angel and Devon's life, Frankie had yet to act upon it. Much to his chagrin, he was starting to realize Dino's observation that the two were worth much more to him if they were alive, afraid and under his control, was in fact absolutely accurate. Frankie knocked back his rye and gestured to Devon. "Want another?"

Devon looked down at the full glass of liquor in front of him. He had to keep a clear head. "No thank you, Frankie. I have a nice bottle of scotch at home. But I do appreciate your hospitality."

Frankie grinned. Devon was strange and fascinating to him. He seemed so out of place in the world of organized crime, and yet the mob boss was starting to learn they had more in common than he initially presumed.

"Alright, Devon. Let's talk details."

Lights Out

After leaving Devon's suite, Angel made her way down the main drag into Rale's entertainment district, her gun holster slung around her shoulders. It was the time of the evening when the nightlife was quietening down, bars were closing their doors and club owners were counting their profits for the night. At the same time as weary partygoers made their way home, Angel relished the emptying of the streets. It signalled it was time for her to get to work.

She rounded the corner and her target's nightspot came into view. It would be an easy job. He owed money to the London-born mobsters who owned that particular patch on club row. She would intimidate and humiliate him, he would hand her the cash, she would take a 10% cut and return the remaining profits to the Cockney gang member who hired her. Easy money. Only tonight, something felt different. It felt... *off*. Devon had acted peculiarly, and the assassin had an uneasy feeling in the pit of her stomach.

As she mulled over the feeling, Angel sensed a large shadow engulfing her and, before she could react, she felt a strong arm around her neck with the other hand covering her mouth. She screamed. The sound muffled against his leather gloves.

She felt a needle pierce the flesh on her neck. Everything went black.

Sometime later – she assumed several hours but she really had no idea – she opened her eyes. Angel felt completely out of it at first. Groggy. She turned her head in an attempt to calculate her whereabouts, but soon realized there was a barrier in front of her sightline. One dazed moment later, the usually sharp assassin realized she had a thick clothed hood over her head.

"At last, you're awake," she heard a man mutter. His voice was quiet but the tone vibrated around the open space. This informed Angel that wherever she was, it was large and empty. The sound of footsteps on concrete became louder as he walked towards her, and once again she felt her frame swallowed in a shadow. He pulled off the hessian sack in a swift upwards motion and suddenly she could see. She took a huge gulp of air.

Her captor rested his hands on his knees as he stood in front of her, bending over so their eyes were level. She couldn't distinguish his features, his face disguised by a thick black balaclava. Angel could tell he was tall and lean. His suit was crisp. Tailored. He stood upright and walked to the corner of the room towards two loaded automatic weapons, excessive firepower considering the pistol he already held in his hands.

Angel soon realized she was tied securely to a chair in a large, empty warehouse. It was derelict and looked similar to a disused aircraft hangar. The roof towered 50 feet above her and the murky windows at the top of the walls let in only thick streams of foggy light, penetrating an otherwise dark and gloomy space. It wasn't the warehouse she knew so well – it was a different place. But everything about it said professional mobster – it was the perfect location to hold a target hostage. Her captor was now heavily armed, pointing his automatic weapon purposefully in her direction.

He noticed Angel surveying her surroundings and he turned his head to the door. He looked back to her and shook his head once, twice. No. She wasn't going anywhere. He walked back towards her and her defenses kicked in.

"I know who hired you! I fucking know!!" she screamed, shaking her bound wrists, tied behind her back in a methodical prisoner loop and secured once more to the rails of the chair's back. She gulped down hard, her throat dry as he moved in closer, his face now inches from hers. *This is how my targets feel*, she thought, the fear paralysing her. He used the barrel of his semi-automatic to poke her in the shoulder. He didn't say anything. He didn't have to.

She knew what was happening. She fully understood that the chances of a seasoned mobster *accidentally* kidnapping the city's top assassin – who was currently locked in a battle with Rale's mob boss while simultaneously dating the city's top entrepreneur – were slim, to say the least.

She could continue fighting and showing her aggression. She could tell him what she knew. *But why give away all my power*, she thought. She knew exactly what to do to take control and this situation was no different.

This isn't going to be too complicated.

"Baby... you have the most beautiful eyes," she purred in the sweetest tone she could muster. She didn't care how forced it sounded. Her life was on the line.

He laughed. A deep, throaty, dirty laugh. "Thank you, beautiful." Internally she shuddered. Externally she didn't miss a beat. She smiled as his hand stroked the side of her face and his eyes roamed all over her fit, athletic body.

As she flirted back and forth with her captor and maintained eye contact, slowly, carefully she lifted her right leg up behind her. With her hands tied, she was able to reach the handle of the switch blade she kept hidden in the leg of her knee-high leather boots. She hid it there for exactly this reason. She never told Devon. It wasn't that she wanted to deceive him, but if he didn't know about the weapon then the information couldn't be coerced out of him under duress. Frankie knew about it. That was one person too many.

She pulled the switch blade out by its handle and waited for her abductor's turn to speak again. His voice, though muffled by his balaclava, seemed familiar to her. As soon as he uttered a little volume, she released the switch blade, his words disguising the sound. Angel held her knife carefully by the handle and slowly whittled away at the ropes binding her hands to the chair.

Ropes, she thought. *Interesting. Any lawbreaker worth his salt is using cable ties. Amateurs.*

Soon, the ropes came undone and fell away in her hands. She held the rope in place, hands remaining behind her back. She decided to wait for the moment to strike. It could take minutes or hours, but Angel felt confident in her position now that she was ready to make a move when the opportunity presented itself.

"Mmmm..." she moaned, as she leaned forward to breathe in his scent. "You smell good, baby."

All of a sudden, a memory triggered in her mind. Something about this man's smell reminded her of Devon. It wasn't Devon's cologne. *No*. But it was an aroma that was familiar to her. Her mind sharpened the memory. She had always possessed an uncanny ability to connect smells to memories. There were times Angel would catch wafts of cologne from a man walking past her in the street and it would bring forth a tsunami of memories. Usually, they were recollections she had buried deep down and would much prefer they stay hidden from view.

Yes, she knew this scent. It was present when Devon's security detail stood with him. She observed the tall man in front her. *Yes. It's him.* She knew exactly who her captor was. What she didn't know was *why*.

"You know, your cologne is so... familiar... to me," she started. Through the holes in the balaclava, Angel noticed his pupils dilate. *He knew that she knew.* "Is there something you want to tell me, baby...?"

His hands tightened on his weapon and in an instant she whipped her hands forward, her switch blade in her right hand as she pushed him to the ground. Angel straddled him and pressed her knife against his neck. An ounce of pressure and he would bleed out onto the cold concrete in a matter of minutes.

"Where is he? Where's Devon?"

No reply.

"WHAT HAVE YOU DONE WITH HIM??" she screamed, ripping off his balaclava with her free hand. He held his hands up, pleading with her not to kill him. But still he hadn't answered her.

"Look Will, I've always liked you and I don't want to hurt you, but if you've done ANYTHING to Devon, I swear I'll end your life right here. No regrets."

"He's fine! He's fine! He is, I promise you!" Will replied quickly, his arms remaining up in defense as his hands shook. So if Will hadn't conjured up this entire scheme to hurt Devon, why the hell had he captured her? It didn't make any sense.

"I would be doing you a favour by killing you," Angel reasoned. "Because when Devon finds out you did this to me, he'll go absolutely nuts. I can't even imagine how he'll make you suffer. It really would be better if I ended it right here and now, I –"

"*He* did it! Devon did it! He gave the order!" Will spluttered.

Angel's blood ran cold. Dumbstruck, she slowly moved the knife away from Will's neck and loosened her grip on him.

"D-Devon...? Devon did this?" she asked quietly, barely able to say the words out loud.

Will simply offered a sad smile and a shrug. Angel couldn't wrap her head around it.

"Frankie," she said suddenly. "He had you capture me because he's going to go talk to Frankie. Son of a –"

Without another word she jumped off Will and fled the warehouse.

"Angel," Will called after her, his voice inaudible as the wind whisked past her ears in the fresh air outside. "He was trying to protect you. We all were. I'm sorry for what I did to you. I'm so very sorry. It was part of the plan."

Outside now, she looked around. She found herself at the port side of the warehouse district. She spotted one of Devon's town cars nearby and hotwired it, driving it back to Devon's tower, absolutely furious the entire way.

* * *

"So let me get this straight," Frankie started, pouring another glass of rye after hearing Devon's tale. "You've had your guy kidnap Ange and she's tied up somewhere? Right now?"

"Yes, that's right. I told you there was more to me than meets the eye," he grinned slyly. "Of course, you may want to think about how best to take advantage of this opportunity. If you would like to think about it, perhaps you could call me in an hour?"

Devon placed down his business card. Frankie's eyes fell to the stark white cardstock before he looked back up at Devon. *Is this guy for real?*

"Frankie, thank you ever so much for your time. It's been a pleasure," Devon smiled, placing down the full glass of rye full with barely a drop of it sipped. "Would you mind if I exited out of the back entrance? If I'm seen leaving your manor, it may raise suspicion of our plan to join forces."

Frankie nodded, standing as he shook the blond's hand. He watched Devon walk towards the door and the crime lord grinned wickedly. Finally, he would have full control over Angel. At long last.

Devon stopped. It was time to execute the final element of his plan.

On his way towards the door, he glanced over his shoulder at the mobster. Frankie smiled and bowed his head as a mark of respect towards his new ally. His smile started to fall as he watched Devon turn around and pull the silver pistol from the inside pocket of his custom-made suit. The financial mogul showed no expression as slowly, purposefully, he walked towards the crime boss, held out the gun and pointed the barrel directly at his target.

Devon pulled the trigger, shooting Frankie in the heart.

Bang. Bang. BANG BANG BANG.

Five shots.

Frankie's eyes widened, the pain overwhelming him. He clutched his chest and attempted to splutter out for help. No words came. The mobster fell backwards into the side of his chair and slid to the ground.

His face expressionless, Devon's arm fell and the

smoking weapon lost the view of the target from its crosshairs. Devon was numb. He stood there, staring. He knew he needed to turn and make a rapid exit but he had the urge to deliver one last message. He stood over Frankie, his face chillingly void of emotion.

"You hurt her. So you had to go."

The criminal's breathing became laboured and Devon watched coldly as his victim drew his last breath, blood now seeping into the rug below him. Hearing footsteps out in the hallway, Frankie's goons overhearing the gunshot, he sprinted out of the back exit and into his awaiting town car. Mike was already sat at the wheel of the vehicle with the engine running as planned. Devon opened the car door and jumped into the back seat, lying down and closing the door as the car prepared to speed off on the gravel driveway.

"Go, Mike! GO!" Devon demanded as his security slammed his foot on the gas, gravel making the tires spin before the car lurched into motion.

Gunshots echoed around the vehicle as Frankie's men shot at them, broken glass raining down onto Devon. He leaned out of the back window and fired at Cucinotta's goons.

"Are you fucking nuts boss? Get down!" Mike screamed as he steered them away from danger.

The financier continued shooting, hitting one of the mobsters in the arm. It bought Devon and his aide a couple seconds free from bullets. They made it out onto the main road and Mike continued to drive at breakneck speed until they reached the bridge into the city.

They had made it.

Battle for Control

Back at his suite, Devon washed the sins of the night from his body. His fine tailored clothing, speckled with blood spatter, lay on the tiles of his pristine bathroom floor. The water rushed over his naked form and he brushed his hair back with his hands, running the soap through his locks.

He thought of what he did. How he had killed in cold blood. How he escaped with his life. How he was able to execute a complex plan flawlessly and keep Angel in the dark about the whole set-up. Was he really that calculated? That good of a liar? It chilled him.

Who am I becoming? Is this who I've been all along?

He was thankful Mike escaped unscathed. The last thing he wanted was for one of his men to get hurt during the breakout from Frankie's manor. Immediately after they sped away from the scene, Mike advised they drive in a loop around the Greater Rale Area, buying time and ensuring Frankie's goons were not on their tail. When they arrived back at the private underground parkade, Devon leaned through to the front of the car, resting his hands on the back of the two headrests. "What now, Mike? What do you advise?"

"You mean Frankie's guys? Will they come after you?"

"Yes."

"Nah. It's been a couple hours now. If they were gonna kill you, you would be dead already. My guess is they're battling for who's taking his place. My money's on Dino. Would be good for you, from what you said."

"Yes. Dino was rather kind, as it happens. You were right, he has an affection for Angel."

"Not too much, I hope boss."

"No, it seemed platonic. He appeared like an older brother. Besides, I highly doubt he would dare cross me now. He's seen how I took care of his predecessor."

"You sound like a mob boss," Mike smirked. Devon raised his eyebrows. He *did.* He thought about it, allowing the idea to settle. One thing was certain – he had a trusted friend in Mike.

"Thank you, Mike," Devon said after a brief pause. "Thank you for everything. You risked a great deal for Angel's safety. Thank you."

He nodded and patted Devon's shoulder. "Anytime boss. Would do it again. No trouble."

Despite Devon's insistence that Mike take the day off to rest and recuperate, he stubbornly insisted on standing guard outside of his boss' suite.

And here Devon found himself in the shower, thinking over his next steps. What would he tell Angel? He had to inform her of Frankie's demise, and the anticipation created a warm sensation in his stomach. *She will feel incredibly relieved*, he mused. She wasn't due to return from her capture for quite some time, having instructed Will to keep her for up to 12 hours as contingency. Devon hadn't felt certain of the fallout following Frankie's death and wanted to ensure she was safe rather than exposing her to the risk of being caught in the crossfire.

What would he tell her? She was smart. She would know it was an extremely unlikely coincidence to be kidnapped on the same night Devon assassinated the leader of Rale's criminal underworld. But telling her... telling her *he* was the one who caused her so much pain, so much fear... it was almost too much for him to bear. It weighed so heavily in his heart. He betrayed her. He did it *for* her, but it was still a betrayal. If he didn't tell her the truth now, the lie would sour over time like bad milk. He was conflicted.

Stepping out of the shower, he dressed in a clean suit as if it were business as usual.

After all, the sun was rising on a new day in Rale. He had an empire to run.

* * *

Angel pushed the elevator button repeatedly.

"C'mon, c'mon...!!" she said urgently, glancing back at the large grandfather clock in the hallway. 5am.

"Oh, fuck it!" She ran towards the emergency stairwell to make her way up, before hearing the *ding* of the elevator. "Fuck!!" she cursed as she hurried back across the hallway to the bank of elevators.

She was frantic. The elevator couldn't carry her fast enough. Reaching his floor, she burst through the front doors of the suite. She found all of the lights on.

"Devon! Devon, where are you?" she yelled, searching the main living space of the suite. He wasn't there. "Where the fuck are you?!" she shouted again, poking her head around the bedroom door. Nothing. Finally, she rounded the corner of his study and found him stood nursing a glass of Glenn Dearg, one hand resting in his pocket. He turned around and his face beamed when he saw her. "Angel, you're safe, I was so worried –"

"You fucking idiot!" she said, pushing him in the chest as he took a step back to steady himself. "Having me kidnapped, who the fuck does that! You're not going to talk to Frankie, he'll kill you!!"

"My dear, w-whatever do you mean, I –"

"Cut the crap, Devon. I know it was you. Hey, next

time you have one of your guys capture me, tell him not to wear his fucking cologne!" she shouted. "The ropes were a dead giveaway, too. Nobody uses ropes anymore. Everyone knows I only use them for show."

"Amateurs." He shook his head, unaware his words mirrored those of the woman in front of him earlier that night. "Besides, those new plastic ties are ghastly, I hear they leave terrible marks, and –" he stopped, noticing her blank expression. Like him, her anger tended to start on a simmer and lead to a full boil. While she appeared reasonably together on the surface, underneath her rage was bubbling up like a volcano. "Never mind. The main thing is that you're unharmed."

"No, Devon," she barked, "The 'main thing' is that *you* were the one who fucking kidnapped me! How could you do that to me? I trusted you!"

Despite his best efforts against the truth, he decided to come clean. "Yes, I kept it from you. But I had to. Ever since Frankie attacked you, I knew I had to act. I planned it for quite some time. It took an enormous level of attention to detail, I assure you. And allowing my two best men offsite to plan this, leaving me with only George for protection, was certainly not a decision I made lightly. But, well I... I did it for... for... love."

"Love?!" Angel bellowed, her hands gesturing angrily at her sides. "You call this *love*?"

"My dear, please, allow me to explain further, I –"

"Are you fucking crazy?!" she exclaimed. As soon as those last four words left her lips she wanted to take them back. Desperately she chased the words through the air, but they reached his ears. It was too late.

He sat down now, his hand propping up his face. He didn't look angry. He appeared sad. Empty. He looked at the rich carpeting beneath him as he explained, "I was concerned you would think that of me. What kind of person kills in cold blood? I am a monster, truly. But I simply couldn't allow him to continue, Angel. Not after what he did to you. I couldn't accept you living in fear."

She remained quiet. Her mind was so numb she couldn't process his words. He assumed the worst.

"How could I possibly think I could have a relationship? Especially with a woman as incredible as you. Perhaps it is my destiny to live my life alone. I don't deserve anything more, especially with the unspeakable things I've done." He looked down at his hands, clasped in front of him, resting on his lap. He wiped away a single tear falling onto his handsome face. His blue eyes looked hollow, cold. "Before tonight, I treated people terribly. The things I did to women, the way I used them. It's atrocious. So if you want to walk away, I'll understand. Besides. I didn't do this for *us*. I did it for *you*. To free you."

He looked at her now. She walked towards him and sat down beside him. She spoke gently, her own emotions softened by his declaration.

"Do you know how afraid I was? I thought it was Frankie. I was so scared of what he was going to do to me, Devon. I was terrified."

"I know you must have been afraid. And believe me, I felt sick thinking of how you must feel. But I couldn't risk you getting hurt during all of this."

Angel stood there, dumbfounded. His tirade had put her on an emotional rollercoaster for the past several minutes. As stunned as she was, something clicked. In an instant she understood his motivations.

"It wasn't so I didn't stop you talking to Frankie. It was for my safety," she stated. It wasn't a question, but rather her thoughts coming together out loud as she pieced together the complexity of the evening's events. "You needed to know I'd be safe, so you had me kidnapped. I see that now. What I don't understand is *why*. Why you had to keep me safe if all you planned to do was talk to him."

He let out a low laugh that momentarily sent a chill down Angel's spine. "Isn't it obvious?"

"No," she said simply. Truthfully, Angel had an inkling but she had to hear him say the words before she would believe it.

She took his hands and held them in hers, placing them softly in her lap.

"What did you do, Devon?"

"I paid Frankie a visit at his residence. We talked. It's already done," he said simply.

He looked up at her, his blue eyes glassy. He paused.

"You needn't be afraid. He can't hurt you anymore, Angel."

"W-what do you mean?" Angel asked, her usually strong diction wavering.

"I took care of it."

There was no emotion in his voice. None.

"What...?" She detected the dark tone laced in his words but refused to believe Devon was capable of such a thing.

He looked down at the table, then back up at her. He swallowed hard.

"I killed him Angel. He's gone."

"N-no," she started, standing up, her fingers trembling as she covered her mouth with her hand. "N-no, you can't have killed him – you're not like that. You *couldn't*. No. He can't be dead, I-I..."

Devon's brows furrowed in confusion. He hadn't anticipated instant praise from Angel, but her reaction was so hard to gauge that he truly didn't know whether she was thrilled at the crime lord's demise, or devastated with a feeling of profound loss.

She looked down at the ground and shook her head in disbelief, her mind processing the events of the evening. She looked up at him. "H-he's gone? He's really gone?" Devon nodded. Angel started to cry, tears of relief falling fast down her cheeks. "Oh God, oh thank God... it's over, it's finally over..."

Devon stood up to catch her and she collapsed into him, her sobs echoing through the room. Devon held her tight, his arms soothingly rubbing her back. "Shh. It's okay. He's gone. You don't have to worry. It's just you and I now."

"I don't know what to say. You did that for me?" the assassin choked out. He nodded. "Thank you Devon. Thank you, thank you..."

He pulled her body towards him and wrapped his arms around her tightly. She never asked him to do this. She didn't think he was capable of it and, more than that, she would never place him in such danger. But gratitude leaked from her every pore. Her only fear now was the genuine concern of never feeling able to fully express her appreciation. He risked his life for her. For her honour. For her freedom.

"I..." he swallowed, the emotion caught in his throat, and looked up her. "I... I love you, Angel."

She looked up into his blue eyes, the feeling of affection washing through her caused her heart to swell. The sensation consumed her, and as the seconds ticked by she realized she had yet to vocalize her thoughts. How she would articulate her feelings, she had no idea. So she spoke from the heart.

"I love you Devon. I can never repay you for what you've done for me. I'm so grateful to you. I love you, I love you so much –"

The sentence was cut short by her lips crashing into his.

She worked on removing his tie, eager to engage in

their familiar fun and games. Devon stopped her.

"Angel," he said between kisses. "Not yet. First, there's something I would like to propose."

Angel immediately leaped back, her sharp wit returning. "If you get down on one knee, as much as I love you Devon, I *will* kick you in the balls."

Devon stifled a laugh and retorted, "My dear, I will drop to my knees any time you command me to. Although, no, I'm not asking for your hand in marriage. But there is something I must ask of you."

Angel narrowed her eyes and titled her head ever so slightly. *What on earth was he up to now?*

"Well. Here goes. I confess, I'm not sure how to articulate this. But... I want everyone to know we're together. No more sneaking around. No covert operations. No more of this *'Angel is an urban legend'* talk. I want you to step into the light, so to speak. I want people to know you're real, you're wonderful, and we're in this together."

Angel couldn't stop the smile spreading across her face, and she didn't even try.

"I would be okay with that," she grinned widely, her eyes not leaving his.

"That makes me very happy, Angel. *You* make me very happy."

"I quite like you, as well," she grinned. She held out her hand and gestured towards his neck tie.

Without saying a word, he removed it and handed it to her.

"Up," she commanded, as he raised his hands above his head and she tied his wrists together. "Sit down. Now."

His tongue lapped at the corner of his mouth in anticipation of what was to come.

"Yes, miss."

Acknowledgements

I'm overwhelmed with gratitude to all of my loved ones for their incredible support during the creation of *Angel of the Night*. There are so many people I want to mention. Forgive me if you're not listed here. You are in my heart and I appreciate you.

Thank you to my brother Dean. To my Mum and Trevor. To my Dad and Sue (and Louis!). I love you all. To my cat-dog Mowgli, who sat beside me during many a late-night writing session. To my extended family, particularly my Auntie Ros. To my friends, especially Helen, Kim and Jennifer. Thank you for being there when the road felt rocky. To my fan fiction sisters who made me realize writing kink was not only okay, but it was encouraged! To my assistant Erin for keeping me sane. To Olivia for your unwavering belief in me when mine wavered (especially then). To Alisia Leavitt of Alisia Leavitt Media for your editing prowess and your deep understanding of these characters. And finally, to the incredible team at Rowanvale for your love and dedication to this project.

No woman succeeds in isolation. Thank you all for lifting me up.

About the Author

Cheryl J. Muir was born in Britain but has lived in three countries and holds both British and Canadian citizenship. A former corporate professional, Cheryl quit her day job in September 2014 in order to set up her own business.

Angel of the Night: The Monster Within is Cheryl's first published book. The idea for the novel was conceived in Cheryl's apartment in Vancouver when she was coming out of a deep depression following a car accident. Cheryl travelled extensively while completing her debut novel, writing in several locations in America, Canada and England. Rale, the fictional city in which Angel of the Night takes place, is inspired by several cities that have touched Cheryl's heart over the years: New York City in the U.S., New Westminster in Canada, and Manchester and London in England.

You can learn more about Cheryl on her website www.cherylmuir.com. You can also connect with Cheryl on Twitter using her handle @cheryljmuir.

Publisher Information

Rowanvale Books provides publishing services to independent authors, writers and poets all over the globe. We deliver a personal, honest and efficient service that allows authors to see their work published, while remaining in control of the process and retaining their creativity. By making publishing services available to authors in a cost-effective and ethical way, we at Rowanvale Books hope to ensure that the local, national and international community benefits from a steady stream of good quality literature.

For more information about us, our authors or our publications, please get in touch.

www.rowanvalebooks.com
info@rowanvalebooks.com

Lightning Source UK Ltd.
Milton Keynes UK
UKOW01f1817170217
294694UK00004B/198/P

9 781910 832554